Husband Swap & Roughing It: Two Dirty Stories

Kelly Carr

Also by Kelly Carr:

Male/Female/Male
Romantic Hedonism

Husband Swap & Roughing It: Two Dirty Stories

Kelly Carr

New Tradition Books

Husband Swap and Roughing It: Two Dirty Stories
by
Kelly Carr

New Tradition Books
ISBN 1932420738

For information contact:
New Tradition Books
newtraditionbooks@yahoo.com

Dirty Story Number One:

Husband Swap

The other man.

As he opened the hotel door, I said, "I've got something for you."

He leaned back and gave me a good once over, smiling at my short black trench coat and stilettos. "I think I might like something like that."

I wriggled my eyebrows and said, "So come and get it."

He grabbed me, pulled me into the room and threw me up against the wall and pressed his lips on top of mine. Ahh, yeah! That felt so good. Shocks of delight snaked up and down my body, sending goosebumps out to cover my skin.

"Mmm," I moaned and licked at his lips.

"You taste so good," he moaned back and tore the coat open. He stepped back and stared at me.

"What is it?" I asked and looked down.

"Kara, you're naked under there!" he exclaimed.

"Well, yeah, that's the point, Cole."

"I like that," he said and ran his hands up and down my body. "God, your body is so sexy."

I smiled with satisfaction; it should be sexy, too. I worked out enough for it to be. And I watched every morsel I put into my mouth. The sacrifice had paid off. I was sexy to this man right in front of me. And he was sexy to me.

"Such a tight little body," he said and began to paw at me like I was his plaything. And, I suppose, I was. He was certainly mine.

I stood there and writhed as he manhandled me, as he grabbed at my tits and stuck his hand between my legs. I ground against it for a moment until he got down on his knees and pushed his head between my legs. I gasped. This was going to be *so* good. I threw one leg over his shoulder and moved against the wall as he began to eat at me. He didn't hesitate either. He went in with gusto, with all he had. He used his lips to suck at my pussy and he used his fingers to explore and arouse me. He used his nose to tease my clit, rubbing up against it so that I could have come just like *that.*

"Ooh," I moaned. "I'm gonna come!"

"Come on, baby," he murmured and looked up at me. "Come on and do it."

I grabbed onto his head and ground myself against it. He clamped his mouth on my pussy and began to suck at it. The orgasm just came at me then, attacking me with delight. It made me weak but it made me strong, too. It made me want more and more orgasm, to make me feel alive.

"Mmm," I moaned as he kissed his way up my body and to my mouth. "You're good."

"Mmm," he moaned back. "I've been thinking about doing that to you all day."

I smiled at him. "Really?"

He nodded. "Really. I can't wait to fuck you."

"Then get to it."

He got to it. But he started slow, licking at my lips until I opened my mouth to receive his kiss, then he picked me up, walked me to the bed and threw me down. I lay there and panted as he kissed me and began to pull his clothes off, wanting him naked, wanting his cock in me so bad. Wanting him to fuck me six ways to Sunday.

Soon he was naked and was pressing against my body. I wrapped my legs around his waist and kissed him. He kissed back for a moment before turning me over onto my stomach. Oh, yeah, doggie. He liked doing it like that. He liked taking me from behind, fucking my brains out as he did so. I liked it, too.

I got up on all fours and he got behind me, pushed my legs together and then pushed his cock into my wet and wanting pussy. I gasped a little when he shoved it in. The pressure was always too much at first, but never too much to take. He began to ride me, grabbing onto my hips and pulling them back as he rocked me. I went with him and enjoyed the sensations of his cock and of being in the moment, this intense sexual moment. It was all about the fucking with us.

He leaned over and put his hand between my legs, then sucked on my neck. I shivered in delight and began to ride his hand. It didn't take a second before I got my groove on. He did that to me. He always knew how to make me come. Always knew how to get me going and to keep me going.

I felt it then; I felt the orgasm. It came at me and made me dance against him, made me want him to give it to me harder, with a little more viciousness. I liked it dirty and I wanted him to deliver. He did and started to fuck me so hard, my head slammed into the headboard. I clawed at it and at the sheet as I came. It was a long one and it made me moan aloud, so loud that I was sure the people in the next room could hear me. But I didn't care. It had to be released; otherwise I wouldn't have been take to take it.

Just as he came, he pulled out. I turned over and he squirted his hot white cum all over my breasts. I shivered and gyrated as it hit me. It felt so good and dirty. He loved doing that. I loved for him to do it. I wanted more, so I turned around and grabbed onto his cock, took it into my mouth and finished him off. Once I was done, he bent down and kissed me, thrusting his tongue into my mouth where I sucked on it until he moaned and fell on the bed.

I fell beside him and he pulled me into his arms, spooning me, and kissed my shoulder. I could feel his semi-hard cock pressing against my leg. I could hardly wait for it to reach its full potential again. Ahh, good sex, nothing like it in the whole world. I smiled, feeling very loved and very satisfied. I loved feeling this way.

"I've said it once," he muttered and kissed my neck. "And I'll say it again. You're the best fuck I've ever had."

"Thanks," I said.

He looked over my shoulder at me and said, "God, you're so beautiful."

"You're so good with that shit," I said and felt warmth in my cheeks.

"But you are."

I glanced over at the mirror and thought, *Maybe he's right.* I'd never thought about the way I looked. I knew I looked good, but then again, so did a lot of other people. I kept my hair long and dark, the color I was born with. I never wore make-up and my skin had freckles scattered here and there. It was tanned and smooth thanks to the care I took of it. My eyes were nice, probably my best feature. They were blue and dark, long eyelashes framed them. I hated my nose. It was longer than I would have liked and a little rounded on the tip. Cole thought it was cute. I thought it was hideous.

"Don't touch that nose," he'd said once when I mentioned wanting to get a nose job. "It's perfect."

"No, it's not," I said. "It's crooked where my sister hit me with a basketball."

"Leave it alone."

Well, if *he* insisted. He. Cole. Him. I rolled over and stared at him. He stared back and smiled slightly. He was so great, so good looking and tall and manly. He was nearly six-foot-one. I was almost a foot shorter than he was. He was so big, he made me feel even smaller and more delicate, like a little doll. He was so great but, he didn't belong to me, other than in this capacity. He was another woman's husband. I was an adulteress. He was the other man in my life and he belonged to another woman. I was with her man.

But so what? She was with mine.

Lily.

It should be noted that I didn't even want to go to this stupid party. The hostess was an old acquaintance of mine but I hadn't seen her in years. However, one day, out of the blue, I got a call from her and an invitation to her party. My husband really wanted to get out of the house on a Saturday night. However, once we were there, I wished I'd stayed home. I didn't know anyone but the hostess and my husband was dying to play pool in the other room. The house, though, was beautiful and I marveled at it's grandeur for a moment, wondering what it would be like to have such a huge house. My old friend had certainly done well for herself. But then, my husband started out of the room again, threatening to leave me standing alone, looking like some idiot.

"Neil," I hissed. "You better not leave me here!"

"I'll be back in a few seconds," he said and kissed my temple. "I just want to play one set of pool. After that I promise I'll be right back."

"I mean it," I hissed. "Don't leave me!"

"Be right back," he said, ignoring me and exiting the room.

If I had a knife, I would have thrown it at his back. But I didn't. So I had to stand in a corner of the large room and watch everyone else have fun at the party. I hated parties. I don't even know how I'd gotten duped into attending this one.

I grabbed a champagne flute off a tray from a passing waiter and knocked it back. That was better. If I could get a little drunk, this place might start to warm up. I looked around at all the business suited people and realized it would never warm up. They were all so stuffy and standoffish.

I had a sudden urge to do something, something wild like flashing my tits at all these wet blankets. Something crazy like yelling at the top of my lungs about how fucking beautiful the moon was tonight. Something that might embarrass my husband. Then we'd get to leave. But no, I was a good little wife and good little wife is...well, she's good.

I hated being good. I especially hated being good here. All the people were just so...*ick.* They were *ick.* They were older than me and they were tired looking and too damned stuffy.

But not all of them. Oh, hello there, Mr. Man. He'd been eying me all night and I'd been eying him. Now that my lame husband was gone, maybe he'd talk to me. Maybe not. I shook myself but couldn't help but smile in his direction and turn my heel in a little. He was fine. He was tall with a wide chest and big arms. His hair was a shade or two lighter than my own and his face was sculpted looking with nice lips, strong lips. His lips looked like they knew how to kiss a woman, kiss her hard and throw her down and... Damn! With guys like that around, it sucked to be married and banned from them. It sucked, sometimes, just to be married. The only thing I could do about it, besides nothing, was get a divorce. And who wanted to bother with that? I shuddered at the thought of having to split our assets and all that other crap you have to do.

He left the room. Shit. What was I going to look at now? Oh, the buffet table.

I walked over, smiling at a few people as though I actually liked being there, then took a look at all the food. There was a lot there and nothing that I particularity wanted. It was all seafood stuff like oysters—yuck!—and cocktail shrimp and… Oh, my God, they had crawdads! Mud bugs! No way and no thank you. I did not want to suck the head off a hard shelled little creature tonight. I hated seafood.

Screw it. I'd make Cole stop at Burger Hut on the way home.

Just then, a woman about my height, size and age walked up to the buffet table. She was very attractive with dark brown highlighted hair, a pretty face and thin body. She was dressed in this killer black dress and stilettos just like the ones I had on. How funny and how very odd.

I nodded at her and moved a little so she could grab a plate. But what could I do now? I could go back to my corner or I could try to socialize. I looked at the corner. It was very inviting but I'd been standing there all night. I was sick of it, too. I hadn't wanted to come but Neil said it would be "good" for us to get out of the house on a Saturday night. It would be good, perhaps, if we weren't at a party with a bunch of stiffs and if I was in the mood to socialize, which I wasn't. I was in the throes of PMS and all I could do was hope I could keep the bitch at bay until we left. Then I'd let her out. Neil loved her, loved the PMS bitch. She visited often and made his life a living hell. What's not to like? Actually, he hated her. But then again, so did I.

Sometimes I felt very, very sorry for my husband. Sometimes not. I chuckled to myself. He usually ran whenever I was PMSing. He was a smart man.

The woman was eying me. Oh, no, she wanted to talk. I looked around, trying to find a way to leave the room, but then I looked back at her. She seemed pleasant enough, so I said, "Hi."

"Hello," she said nicely and nodded.

"Having fun?"

She shrugged. "I suppose. You?"

"No."

She threw her head back and laughed loudly, getting a few looks from other people, which she ignored. She leaned in and whispered, "I was just thinking the same thing. I was just thinking abut how *bad* this party was and wondering if it was just me."

"I was wondering the same thing," I said. "I just wrote it off as PMS."

"It's not PMS," she said. "It's this party. It's dead."

"That it is," I said. "But it's a nice party, though."

"Yeah," she said, looking around. "They probably spent a lot of money on it, too."

"Yeah," I said, then, for some reason, added, "I don't know anyone here."

"Me either. I mean, my husband knows the host, he's his boss, but other than that, no." She picked a shrimp off her plate, popped it into her mouth and chewed, then spit it out. "God, this sucks!"

"I don't like seafood that much," I said. "So I didn't try it."

"Smart girl," she muttered and set the plate on the table. "God, I hope I don't get food poisoning off that."

"I hope not, too," I said and sipped my champagne.

"So you don't know anyone here at all?" she asked.

"Oh, I know the hostess," I said.

She nodded for me to continue.

"Anyway, I went to school years ago with her," I said. "I was surprised as hell when she called to invite me to her party."

"Oh yeah?" she said. "Why?"

"I thought she hated me," I said. "She thought I took away her boyfriend or something. It was this whole thing."

"Wow," she muttered. "Did you?"

"Did I what?"

"Take away her boyfriend."

"Oh, yeah," I said. "I took him. I mean, he came to me and it wasn't my fault they were still dating. I later dumped him, though."

"Why?"

"He smelled weird," I said. "It was like he was the cutest guy but he had this funk. And it wasn't boy goat smell either."

"'Boy goat smell'?" she asked with a raised eyebrow.

"Yeah, boy goat smell," I said. "I don't know why they get it or where or how, but young boys get this smell about them. It's like… It's like a goat smell. I guess it's some kind of hormone or something. But they smell like goats. They have a goat smell."

"A goat smell?" she said. "Umm…"

"Well, maybe it was just the boys I knew in school," I said.

"What kind of school did you go to?"

I stared at her. She stared back and then we cracked up. "No, I didn't go to some hillbilly school. God! How could you even think that? But anyway, this dude I supposedly stole from her had a funk, okay? Anytime I was around him, I'd almost gag."

"What did he smell like?" she asked. "I mean, if he didn't smell like a goat, what would he smell like?"

I considered. "He smelled wet."

"Wet?"

"He smelled like he'd put his clothes up wet," I said. "And they'd mildewed but he wore them anyway."

"Eww!"

I nodded. "It sucked. I'd get close to him and want to puke. Then I'd get away from him and see him from afar and he was *so* cute, I'd want to be close to him again. Then I would and it was too much. It was such a waste."

"Really?"

"Yeah," I said. "I didn't go out with him for very long and even considered telling her to take him back."

"I understand that," she said. "Besides, who'd want someone that stinks?"

"Not me," I said. "But anyway, I only think she invited me here because she was so pissed off at me for 'taking' her boyfriend. I think she just wanted me to see how well she was doing and rub my nose in it. But, hey, I gotta hand it to her. Look at this house!"

"It is nice."

"Yeah," I said.

"Women can be such bitches," she said. "But what can you do?"

"Nothing much," I said. "Besides, that was a long damn time ago."

"It is a nice house," she said, looking around. "By the way, I love your shoes."

I kicked my leg out a little and said, "I like yours too."

She laughed and looked down at our shoes. "Yeah. Anyway, would you excuse me for a minute?"

I nodded and stood back so she could cross in front of me, then looked around and noticed Mr. Man was back in the room. He glanced over, gave a quick nod, then looked away quickly. What was up with that? He was so friendly earlier, too. Well, he had a wedding ring on. Nothing I could do, even if I wasn't married, which I was. Damn it. Life was so complicated sometimes.

He was walking out of the room now, but not before glancing at me again and giving me a slight nod. I bit my lip and smiled at him. He smiled a little and started out of the room and then he was at the door and was almost gone. Bye-bye handsome man.

"I'm back," she said. "What are you smiling at?"

And she was back with a new glass of champagne. I wished she'd bought me one. I just shook my head at her.

"No, tell me what it is," she said.

"Oh, nothing," I said, then waved my hand at the guy. "It's just that guy is so cute."

She looked over my shoulder at him and said, "He *is*?"

"Oh, yeah," I said. "I think so."

She shrugged. "That's my husband."

"Oh, shit!" I exclaimed. "I'm sorry, I didn't—"

"Don't sweat it," she said. "I've been with him for most of my adult life. I guess after a while, the cute wears off. I used to think he was really cute. Now, he's just the dude I'm married to."

I stared at her. Good God, she'd just described the way I felt.

"I mean, yeah, whatever, I still love him and all that."

I looked away. I felt that way about Neil, too.

"But," she said. "For every good looking man out there, there's a woman who's tired of him."

I laughed. How true that was.

"Now he," she said and pointed. "Is cute."

I followed her finger and nearly fell over when I saw it was pointed at my husband.

"That's *my* husband!" I screeched.

"No shit!" she screeched back. "Really?"

I nodded. "Isn't that funny? You think my husband is cute, I think yours is cute."

"Yeah," she said. "Too bad we can't trade. Have a new man for a change."

I laughed and nodded. "Yeah, too bad. But then, after a while, we'd be just as sick of them as we are of our old husbands."

"Ain't that the truth?" She turned to me. "That's really your husband?"

I nodded. "Yeah, he really is."

"Wow," she said and gave him the good once over. "Nice ass."

"Your husband has a nice ass, too," I said for good measure.

"He does," she said. "I make him work out."

I turned to her. "Really? I do the same thing to mine!"

She laughed. "Isn't that funny? But anyway, he was starting to slip a few years ago, getting a gut, going flabby. But I got it fixed. I jumped all over his ass."

"I just threatened to let myself go," I said. "I told him, 'If you're going to do it, so am I.' He couldn't get to the gym fast enough."

We laughed.

"So how long have you been married?" I asked.

"Thirteen years," she said, then added wistfully, "It feels like...*thirty*."

I cracked up. "I know what you mean."

"By the way," she said, extending her hand. "I'm Lily."

"I'm Kara," I said and shook her hand. "So, uh, what's your husband's name?"

"Cole," she said. "What's yours?"

"Neil," I said.

"Nice name," she said and glanced at her watch. "Thank God, we can leave now! An hour is long enough to stay, isn't it?"

"I hope so," I said. "'Cause I'm cutting out here in a few minutes, myself."

She nodded. "So how long have you lived in Atlanta?"

"All my life," I said. "We live near Buckhead."

"Nice part of town," she said. "We live closer to Marietta, in this older part of town. We got a great deal on a big old Victorian-type house and have been renovating for the last three or so years. It's almost done. All we have to do is the garage now, thank God."

"Have you always lived here?"

"No," she said. "We moved up from Louisiana about ten years ago when my husband got transferred."

"Cool," I said.

"Listen," she said, putting her glass on the table. "It was really good to meet you, Kara."

"You, too," I said and smiled at her.

"Let's do lunch sometime," she said and dug into her purse, then handed me a business card. "Just give me a call."

"Sure," I said and glanced at the card. "That would be fun."

"I don't work anymore," she said. "But my home number's on there."

"Cool."

"Never know," she said. "We might see some other cute guys."

"That aren't our husbands," I added.

We laughed.

"See ya later," she said.

"See ya," I said and smiled as she walked out of the room and thought about it. It would be nice to meet some cute guys, preferably ones that didn't belong to other women.

Sex business.

I called Lily the next day and we agreed to meet at Miller's, this little diner not too far from my house. Once I got there, I wondered what I was doing calling a woman I'd just met. But how else are you supposed to meet new friends? God, I hoped it wasn't awkward and she didn't turn out to be weird.

As I entered the diner, my anxiety about the whole thing wore off as soon as I spotted her in a booth at the back of the diner, which seemed to be patronized mostly by working men in business suits and work clothes. She smiled and waved me over. I smiled back and was happy I came. I hadn't had a real girlfriend in years, since college.

"Hey, girl," she said. "Love that sweater!"

I looked down at my white cotton turtleneck and said, 'Thanks. Love yours, too."

She ran her hand along the sleeve of her black sweater and said, "Oh, this old thing?"

"Yeah, that old thing," I said and picked up a menu. "So, what's up?"

"Nothing," she said. "By the way, thanks for coming."

"No problem," I said. "What's good here?"

"I don't know," she said. "It's the first time I've been here. I've always wanted to try it and today seemed like the day."

I nodded and glanced over the menu and muttered, "Same old diner food, heavy on fat and calories. I'll think I'll splurge today and have a cheeseburger and fries. Maybe even a milkshake."

"That's a lot of food," she said.

"Yeah, but I can do it if I don't eat for the next week or so," I said and studied the menu.

She cracked up. "I know what you mean. Isn't it awful that everything that tastes good is bad for you?"

"And everything that tastes bad is good for you," I said, nodding. "I mean, I hate salads and fruit."

"Me too," she said. "But I eat them cause, you know, you have to."

"You do?" I asked.

She studied me for a minute, then cracked up. "Oh, you were joking."

"Yeah, I do that from time to time."

She laughed quietly and said, "I don't think I've met anyone like you in a long time."

"Anyone like me?"

"A person with a good sense of humor," she said.

"Oh," I said. "I know what you mean. Most people I run across are such fuddy-duddies. Like at the party. And if you do joke with them, they just look at you like you're crazy."

"Or demented," she said. "But what can you do?"

"Nothing," I said and closed the menu. "I am definitely having the cheeseburger and fries. I might skip the milkshake unless, of course, you'd be willing to split it with me?"

"I can do that."

"Then let's do it," I said and smiled. "What's the fun in life if you can't throw caution to the wind every once in a while?"

She studied me for a moment and nodded slowly. "You're right. Sounds good to me," she said and motioned the waitress, who came, took our orders, then left. "So anyway, tell me a little about yourself."

"Wow," I said. "I don't get asked that much. Let me think for a minute."

She laughed. "I know what you mean. It's like I've done the same old thing for so long, I just take it for granted that no one would be interested."

"Isn't that the truth?" I said, laughing. "But, yeah…uh…just quit a job and I'm taking a little time off. Been married a long damn time to a great guy… Oh! We finally went to Jamaica last year. I'd been wanting to do that for a while."

"Wow, Jamaica," she said and nodded with approval. "I bet that was nice."

"It really was," I said and thought about it, wishing I could go back soon.

Just then the waitress put our drinks on the table. We pulled back and smiled at her and she told us our food would be out shortly.

"Thanks," Lily said to her.

She nodded once and then left.

"It's weird," she said, turning to me. "We're so much alike."

"How's that?"

"We've both been married for a long time," she said. "We've both been in jobs we disliked and now we're both taking breaks."

"You're taking a break, too?"

She nodded and said, "Now, if I could only give smoking up, I'd be a grown-up."

I chuckled and replied, "Yeah, but what's the fun in being a grown-up?"

"I still don't see it," she said. "When you're young, you can't wait to be older and when you get older, you want to be young again."

"Ironic, isn't it?" I said. "Young people play at being older and older people play at being younger."

"That's very astute."

I shook myself. "It is, isn't it? I don't know where the hell that came from."

"It is astute," she said, laughing slightly. "And when you're young, you don't think you'll ever get bored with the love of your life."

My ears pricked up. "What does that mean?"

"Oh, you know what it means," she said. "Otherwise, you wouldn't have been checking out my husband."

My face stung in embarrassment. "I'm sorry about that."

"No, no," she said. "I checked out your husband, too."

"Well, he is cute," I said.

"But boring, right?" she said.

"Not all the time," I said. "It's more like… I don't know how to say this but it's more like one day I woke up and realized, hey, there are a lot of good looking men in the world."

"When did that happen for you?" she asked.

I considered and said, "I don't remember a specific time, but I was in my twenties and just started to notice other men. I didn't lust or anything after them, it was more like, 'He's cute' or whatever."

But it really didn't hit me until I turned thirty and once I hit it, it was like I was going insane. I felt such lust in my body for other men I couldn't stand it. I didn't tell her that, though. Why should I?

She nodded. "But then did you get to the point of… You know?"

"What?" I asked and then smiled at the waitress when she put our food on the table.

"Anything else?" she asked.

"We're good," I told her and smiled. "Thanks."

She smiled back and left us.

Lily ignored her food and whispered, "You know, the point of wanting to…do it?"

"Do what exactly?" I asked.

"Other men," she said.

Oh. *That.* Why was she asking me this? I didn't want to tell her about my fantasies or any of that, so I had to say, "Who says I want to do other men?"

"Oh, come on," she said. "You know you do."

She was right. I did. Even so, I tried to sound nonchalant, "So?"

"So," she said. "Tell me how it makes you feel."

"Crazy," I said.

She laughed. I stared at her, a little taken aback, but she was hinting at something I'd kept hidden from myself. Yeah, I had been at the point of wanting other men so bad I wondered how I could get away with an affair. But I'd never done anything about it, mostly because I was happily married and I knew guys like Neil didn't come around very often. So I pushed those feelings down even though they'd come up ever so often and I'd have to fight them off, then I'd fight with Neil. And then I'd blame it on PMS and hate myself for being so mean. It was a vicious cycle. It did, indeed, drive me crazy. And I, in turn, drove Neil crazy. Funny how that works.

"It drives me crazy, too," she said, nodding. "But what can we do about it?"

"Uh," I muttered and picked up a French fry. "I don't know, Lily. There's nothing we can do about it, is there?"

"Maybe," she said.

"Maybe?" I asked.

"Well, it's better than going crazy, isn't it?" she asked and uncapped the ketchup bottle.

"Anything's better than going crazy," I replied dryly. "I mean, it does drive me crazy and it's hard to fight, but I have a lot to lose."

"Me, too," she said and shook the ketchup bottle. "I fight with it all the time and think I'm going crazy. I mean, literally, I think I'm going to go insane."

Me, too, I thought. Some days I'd have sexual fantasies about other guys so strong I'd get the urge to run out of the house and hump the first guy I saw on the street.

"What is it?" I asked. "I mean, it's like an urge or something."

"It's just hormones," she said offhandedly. "When I was younger, I used to be able to control it more, you know? But once I hit thirty... Well, it's been almost unbearable."

I nodded and took a bite of my burger, chewed and grimaced. The burger was awful. I forced myself to swallow and pushed my plate away. "This burger sucks. I'm not wasting my calories on that."

"Oh," she said. "But, yeah, it became more and more unbearable and the kicker is, I was talking to this older woman I worked with and she said, 'You think it's bad now, girl, just you wait until you turn forty.'"

"What?!" I exclaimed. "It gets worse?"

"According to her it does," she said.

"Fuck," I muttered and really wanted a cigarette, even though I'd quit a while ago. If it got any worse than it was now, I would have to be put away or something. Most days, I could control it, the urge, but there were days where I absolutely thought I was going insane.

"Like I said," she said. "It's all hormones. Nothing we can do about it."

"But go crazy."

"I just wonder sometimes," she said. "If we did it once if it would go away."

"You mean have sex with another man?" I asked.

She nodded eagerly. "Yeah. Just one fuck, that's all, get it all out, be done with it. Then we'd know."

"It would be nice," I said. "And what's one fuck anyway? Everyone should be allowed one fuck in their marriages. I mean one fuck with another man. You can have a fuck with your husband anytime, if you like."

"Exactly," she said and pointed at me with her finger.

Just then, the waitress came by and refilled our tea glasses, then bent over and almost whispered, "I know exactly what you girls are talking about and I can tell you from experience, once you do it once, you have to do it again."

Our mouths dropped.

The waitress nodded at us, then waved her hand around the room, leaned down and whispered, "It's like a dick smorgasbord in here. You think I work here just for the tips?"

I was almost taken aback, but then I realized the diner *was* like a dick smorgasbord. There were all kinds of good looking guys around. Maybe *I* should get a job here.

The waitress stood back up, ripped our check out of her book and said, "If you need anything else, just let me know."

"One thing," Lily said. "How old are you?"

"I just turned forty a few years ago," she said and gave us a sly look. "And that lady who told you it gets worse was right. I've been through three husbands."

I glanced at her nametag and said, "So, tell me, Dena, what can we do?"

"Not a damn thing," she said. "But follow your gut."

Lily and I glanced at each other. I had to ask, "Is it worth it?"

She chuckled at my naïveté. "Oh, yeah, you could say it is."

And with that, she left our table and went over to a group of good looking construction workers and bent over their table. Lily and I stared at each other and cracked up.

We laughed a good five minutes, holding our stomachs and shaking our heads.

“Why doesn’t anyone talk about this stuff?” I asked. “I mean, everyone is thinking it, aren’t they?”

“Everything’s about sex,” she said. “We’re all part of it, it’s the meaning of life but for some reason, it’s a sin and we have to pretend we don’t want it.”

“And that’s bullshit,” I added. “But it does make me feel better knowing I’m not the only one.”

“Me too,” she said and leaned in towards me. “I’ve got an idea.”

“Okay…”

“Why don’t we swap husbands?”

“Wha…?” I muttered, flabbergasted. I mean, yeah, I liked the idea of it all, don’t get me wrong, but I didn’t exactly want to do *that*. I just thought about picking up some random guy, fucking him and then leaving. Besides, I didn’t know if I wanted to share my husband or not. He was mine, after all.

“Oh, come on,” she said. “Don’t act all innocent. I saw the way you were looking at Cole.”

I gave her an indignant look.

“Don’t act like it hasn’t crossed your mind, either.”

“Are you out of your mind?” I screeched.

“Oh, please,” she said. “How old are you?”

“Thirty-four.”

“And how long have you been married?”

“Almost fourteen years,” I replied crisply. “What’s your point?”

“The point is, you’ve been married most of your adult life and you’re acting like you don’t want any strange.”

“Strange?”

“Strange dick,” she said. “I know you do and I know I do. We’ve got good looking husbands so why not do it?”

“Because it’s wrong?” I asked, shaking my head.

“What’s wrong about it?” she said. “I mean, is anything going to change by us doing it or not doing it, for that matter?”

“It’s just… Kinda sleazy.”

“What’s sleazy about it?” she asked. “Aren’t you tired of it, Kara? Aren’t you tired of feeling like you’re losing your mind? I am. I am sick and tired of it. I just want to do it and be done with it once and for all. I mean, why not? I’m so bored. Aren’t you bored, too? Don’t you ever want to throw caution to the wind and do something exciting for a change?”

I shrugged. It still seemed sleazy.

“Listen,” she said. “It makes sense. We know where they’ve been and won’t have to worry about any diseases or any of that other crap. I mean, your husband doesn’t have any diseases, does he?”

“No,” I said and knocked wood.

“Phew,” she said. “Just so you’ll know, mine doesn’t either.”

“Good to know.”

“And anyway,” she continued. “We know they’re good lovers. I mean, your husband is a good lover, isn’t he? Doesn’t premature ejaculate right? He’s not impotent, is he?”

“No!” I exclaimed and knocked wood again.

“Also,” she said. “They’re clean and not on drugs. And besides that, we know they’re in love with us so there are no complications.”

I stared at her. It was almost like she was trying to sell me on the idea. But… But… No! This was ludicrous! It wouldn’t work, for one, and secondly, it wouldn’t work!

“No complications?” I hissed. “You’re asking me to swap husbands! How is that uncomplicated?”

"Because," she said slowly, as if talking to a three year old. "We know each other. I mean, not really, but we know what we like and we know what they like. We also know they're committed to someone else, so we won't have to worry about them getting involved emotionally with us and asking us to leave our husbands."

I knocked on wood again and said, "But the thing is, they might catch on."

"That's the beauty of it!" she exclaimed and pointed her finger at me. "They'll have so much guilt about doing it, it'll eat them up inside."

"Yes!" I exclaimed. She had a point there. That *was* beautiful.

"And the ingenious part is, they'll start treating us better because they're screwing around on us!"

"How's that?"

"Anytime a man cheats, he feels guilt. Or most men do. I know for a fact my husband would. So, when they do it, and because it's 'wrong', they're going to make up for it."

"How?"

"I'd be willing to bet they'll start doing dishes and taking us out to better restaurants and sending us flowers."

"What about some good jewelry? Think we could get that, too?"

"I'm sure of it," she said. "The point is, it's a win-win for everyone. Besides, men are men and eventually both our husbands are going to cheat on us. It's an inevitability. They're both good looking and well mannered, so most women love them. So, if we go ahead and do it now, they will get it out of their systems too and we're all in the clear."

She almost had me hooked, but I couldn't do this. It was absurd! I wanted strange but I didn't know if I wanted it *that* bad.

"I don't know..." I began.

"Listen," she said and leaned in closer. "Cole's got a big dick. I don't know how big your husband's dick is, but Cole's is about eight with width. It's nice. You have to try it out. It's almost like a shame I've kept this thing to myself for so long."

"Oh, shut up!"

"No," she said. "Think about it. How big is your husband's dick?"

"He's about six, I think."

"Six is a good size," she said. "Seven's better, though, but anyway, once you have a big dick, you'll want it again."

"How many big dicks have you had?"

"A couple," she said. "And a few others who weren't so big… But that doesn't matter."

"And it doesn't matter to me what size his dick is," I said. "I mean, my husband is a great lover, if you know what I mean. He's just got a normal-sized dick but he knows how to use it."

"That's the most important thing," she said. "But that's not the point, though."

"You're right," I said. "You're right. They'll never suspect us."

"And we can have some major fun."

I thought about it. The idea was intriguing and her husband was a hunk. But this was all of a sudden. It was too much to comprehend at once.

"Life is too short," she said. "To get hung up. If we could do this and get all the kinks worked out, we could get over this whole sex thing and get on to other things."

"Like what?" I asked.

"Like having kids," she said. "I've put off having kids for years because of this. I want kids, but I want this first, then I can totally concentrate on the kids."

I thought about that. I'd put off kids too, but more on a subconscious level. Kids were great and having a couple might be fun, but until I got over this sex business, I knew I'd go even crazier. She was right. If I could go ahead and do it and get it over with, I'd find out I wasn't missing out on that much and I could commit to a kid.

"So what do you say?" she asked, smiling slightly.

I stared at her and said, "If it all gets fucked up, I don't want to hear about it. If nothing works out, I don't want hear any crying about that, either."

"So you're agreeing?"

I crossed my arms and said, "Yeah. But just once."

She grinned and said, "Just once and then we can pretend it never happened."

"But how can we do it?" I asked. "I don't know your husband and you don't know mine. How can we arrange to meet them?"

"Oh, that's easy," she said. "We can have dinner together."

"No!" I said, my voice rising a little. "I don't think that will work. Besides, it will be awkward as hell."

"You're right," she replied. "Well, you come up with something."

I thought about it for a moment, then said, "How about this? How about we tell them we'll meet at a bar but then you show up at my husband's bar and I show up at yours? That way, we'll meet them in public and if we decided we don't want to go through with it, we won't have to."

"Believe me," she said, "Once that charming bastard starts talking to you, you'll have those panties off in no time."

I just stared at her.

"I'm serious," she said. "I fucked him the first night I met him and I had never done anything like that."

"If he's so charming," I said. "What makes you think he hasn't done it already with someone else?"

"What?"

"Had an affair," I said.

"He better not," she said, shaking her head. "I mean, Cole's not like that. I mean, I know they say all men are the same but he's really not like that. So, I don't think he has. He's been working a lot these past few years and didn't have the time. Now he's the boss and doesn't have to work as much."

"So it's inevitable?" I asked. "I mean, that he'll cheat?"

She considered this. "Probably but, I don't know. I mean, I know he looks at other women but he doesn't make a fool out of himself over them."

"Oh," I said. "Well, neither does Neil."

"Good," she said.

"So, if he's going to cheat, he might as well cheat with me, right?"

"Exactly," she said, "If he's going to screw around on me, I want him to have someone like you."

"What the hell does that mean?"

"You're not skanky," she said. "You're clean and you're married to a very good guy, right? You won't have a hidden agenda. All you're after is the sex."

"Oh," I said. "That makes sense."

She nodded. "I mean, we can't lose. This is every woman's fantasy. We get what we want without having to give anything up."

I hoped she was right about that. I shook myself and said, "Anyway, about the plan. We'll go to the other bars, then call our husbands on their cell phones and tell them we have something that came up."

"Good idea!" she squealed and gave me a high-five. "But we have to do something where they won't have to worry about getting home quick."

I considered and said, "If we worked we could tell them we have to work late."

"But we don't," she said.

"I know," I said. "Shit! Wait! I know! We'll tell them our moms called and needed us to come over."

"My mom doesn't live in town."

"Well, fuck! You think of something."

She considered and said, "I know! We'll tell them there's a big sale going on at Macy's!"

"Yeah, but then they'll bitch about us spending money."

"You're right," she muttered. "Bastards! Listen, you just figure out what you're going to do and I'll figure out what I'm going to. Let's not make it any more complicated than it has to be."

"You're right," I said. "But because they'll be flirting with us, we could pretty much tell them anything. We could tell them we're about to jump off the roof and they'll be like, 'Have fun!'"

She laughed. "You're right, they will! God! This is going to be so much fun!"

I nodded in agreement. "So, we'll go into the bar, hit on them, then they'll take us to a sleazy motel… Slam, bam, thank you ma'am!"

She giggled. "Slam, bam, thank you, ma'am!"

"Wait a minute," I said. "What if they don't bite? What if they're so loyal to us that they won't do anything?"

"Honey," she said. "They're men. Nothing we can do about it, either. You put a bone in front of a dog, he's going to take a nibble."

She was right. All we were doing was putting the bone out.

"What if we ruin our marriages?" I asked and almost panicked. I liked being married. I liked being taken care of. I loved my house!

"Then," she said. "As they say, it wasn't meant to be."

She was right. And it was time to do this thing and let it stop driving me crazy. I asked her, "You've given this a lot of thought, haven't you?"

"I have," she said. "I've been wanting some strange for a long damn time. It's just hard, you know. You don't want to go on the internet and find someone and go to a bar alone… Well, how unsafe is that?"

She was right. It was a lot safer than trying to find a stranger. This might just work out.

"Wait a minute," I said. "What if we're underestimating them? What if they catch on?"

She sighed and said, "Believe me, that's not going to happen."

Slam, bam, thank you, ma'am!

I still don't know how I'd let Lily talk me into this. I was a nervous wreck! Here I was, about to swap husbands and nothing seemed to be going to plan. All I knew was what bar to go to and what Cole looked like. Other than that, everything else seemed to threaten to thwart the plan. Mostly, my husband. God! I had to basically tell him to got to a bar and pick Lily up. Well, I had to tell him to go to the bar to meet me and then when I called to say I couldn't make it, he said, "That's okay. I'll just see you at home."

"No!" I said a little too loudly, a little too quickly. "I mean, don't. You stay and have a beer. You're already there."

"But I don't want to do that," he said. "How pathetic will I look? I'll look like the guy in the bar trying to pick up a woman."

Well, duh, dumbass! I wanted to yell. Like anything like that had never occurred to him! He would *never* be going to a bar to pick someone up. I was handing him a once in a lifetime opportunity and he was too stupid to take it! Then I realized that was because he was very loyal to me. And that made me feel like a complete bitch.

"You're there," I said sweetly. "Have a beer and I'll see you later. I don't know how late I'm going to be but it'll be at least midnight."

"Midnight?" he snapped. "What kind of fucking sale is going on until midnight?"

Being married to someone so long was such a pain in the ass. They knew the exact question to ask and when to ask it. How did anyone get away with cheating? It just didn't seem possible to me. I had a feeling I was going to screw myself good over this one.

"It's a good one," I said quickly, then started babbling to throw him off, "And it doesn't start until later. It's a *best customer* sale. They have those about once a year. Remember last year I went and got that really great black coat? And besides, I need a few good sweaters and everything is on sale. And did you know—"

"So," he said, cutting me off. "I'll just see you at home."

"Yes," I said.

"Well, have fun," he said. "And don't spend too much money."

The next time I saw him, I was going to kick his ass. He was always worrying about me spending too much money. I tried not to seethe as I said, "Okay. Gotta go! Have a drink on me, baby!"

"If you insist," he said. "Love you."

"Love you too," I said and hung up. Phew—fucking—phew! I stared at the bar and wondered just how the hell I was going to pull this off. It was too much work. Too much trouble. Lily's husband better have a big dick or I was going to kick her ass, too.

I got out of the car, then checked myself in the reflection of the window. I looked good. He'd notice me. I had on a short black skirt which showed off my strong and curvy legs and a white top buttoned down to show off my cleavage. I also had on my stilettos. My hair was down and fell onto my shoulders. Maybe I should put it up? That way, he could take it down. *Fuck!* I was putting too much into this. I was over-thinking every little detail. I just needed to go into the bar, sit down, hit on Cole and see what happened.

That's what I'd do. And I really, really needed a drink while I was at it. I squared my shoulders and walked into the bar. It was an up-scale kind of place that had intimate booths and a big bar in the middle. As I walked in, I realized it would be hard to find him because it was so crowded. I glanced at the clock. It was still happy hour. Well, no wonder. Damn it.

I almost panicked when I didn't spot him at first. Where did all these people come from? The bar was full. I went through every head sitting at the full bar and finally spotted him towards the end, sitting face-forward with his eyes on the TV, watching some sort of ball game. My heart fell to my knees. I was really doing this! What was wrong with me? I couldn't do this. It was too crazy, too convoluted.

"Hello, there."

I turned to see a man in a business suit standing next to me stirring his drink with a little straw, which he took out, stuck in his mouth and sucked on. *Nice!*

"I'm Ken," he said.

I just looked at him.

"And you are?" he asked.

"Not interested," I said, remembering how these slime balls never took no for an answer. No wonder I got married so young.

"Let me buy you a drink," he said and smiled. "What would you like?"

I glared at him. Did he think I came in here to hook up or something? Well, I did, but *not* with him. I said crisply, "No thanks."

"C'mon," he said. "Let me buy you a drink."

"No thank you," I said and glanced at Cole. He was sipping his beer, his eyes still glued to the TV.

"Why not?" he asked.

"I don't want your fucking drink, that's why," I hissed and moved to the bar. Life could certainly be a comedy of errors sometimes, couldn't it? I shook my head and decided to call the whole thing off. This was too much to go through just to get some strange. I glanced at Cole. Why did he have to be so cute?

Just then, the seat next to Cole's emptied. It was like a sign. I took it as such and nearly ran to it and hopped up on the stool just in time. He jerked back and stared at me, then his mouth fell open. Play it cool, girl, play it cool. You're just a girl having a drink. That's all. I glanced at him and couldn't help but smile. He was so cute! I could only imagine what he'd look like with his shirt off. His arms were so big and strong looking.

I shook myself and said, "Hi!"

God! That sounded too eager. You can't be eager with a man or they'll get weird and think you want them. And of course, if they think that, then *they* can't want you. Fucking games! I was so glad I was married and didn't have to do this shit anymore.

He shook his head once and said, "Uh…hi."

I smiled and leaned over and looked at his beer. "Is that a good beer?"

He held up his Bud and said, "Uh, I guess."

"I think I'll have one of those," I said and nodded.

He just nodded and looked at the TV. What the fuck?

I motioned to the bartender who got me a beer. Cole sat next to me not saying a word. Maybe he didn't like me. Oh, God! What a fool I was! And now Lily would fuck my husband, thus fucking up my marriage and I wouldn't get squat. I glanced at Cole. Well, if Lily was getting something, I was getting something, too.

I took out a cigarette out of the pack I'd bought on the way over and held it up. It was a good prop, right? He just ignored me. I tried not to growl and searched in my purse for my lighter. This wasn't going to work. Just then, the bartender leaned over, and said, "Sorry, no smoking in here."

"Shit," I muttered and put my cigarette down, wondering how long it had been since I'd been in a bar. A long damn time, apparently.

"I hate that, too," he said. "How's that beer?"

I glanced at the beer, then at him and nodded. "It's fine."

"Let me know if you need anything, okay?" he said.

"I will," I muttered.

He grinned at me, winked and went to wait on another customer. Okay, the bartender was hitting on me but not Cole. What the fuck?

"So," I said, turning to Cole. "How's it going?"

"Fine," he muttered and sipped on his beer.

What a prick! Couldn't he see I was hitting on him? Maybe he could tell I was hitting on him and maybe he didn't want me to. Oh, God! I couldn't do this. I was going to call Lily and call the whole thing off. Then I was going to go home and get on my hands and knees and thank God I was married and didn't have to deal with bars or trying to pick men up. What an idiot I'd been to think this could all work out. What a fool. I had it good and I was willing to throw it all away for some guy. No, that was just stupid. *Stoo-pid*!

I glanced at Cole. He was some guy, that's for sure. Damn, why did he have to be so cute? And those muscles of his were driving me crazy.

"Excuse me," I said and got up.

He didn't even respond. *Prick!* I went to the ladies room, pulled out my cell and dialed Lily. She answered on the third ring.

"Hello," she said.

"Lily," I hissed. "Cole's an asshole!"

"Who is this?"

"It's Kara!" I hissed. "What do you mean 'who is this'? Kara! From the diner?"

"Oh," she said. "Sorry, I just didn't recognize your voice, that's all."

"Anyway," I said. "Your husband is an absolute dick."

"Excuse me?" she said.

I tried not to growl as I said, "Cole, your husband, is a dick."

"What do you mean?"

"He's not falling for me," I said and almost felt like crying. What a waste this had all been. I could be home watching my favorite TV show right now and not here in this stupid bar making an ass out of myself.

"What?!" she exclaimed. "What is he doing? Tell me exactly what he's doing."

"Nothing. That's what he's doing. Nothing," I said. "He won't even talk to me."

She paused before she said, "Oh! No, it's not you."

"What does that mean?"

"It means he's really shy," she said.

Fuck! Of course, I had to the get the guy who was hard to read. And the shy one, too. I hated shy guys; they were such pains in the ass. Neil wasn't shy at all or hard to talk to. Neil was so much better than Cole. I was suddenly glad I was married to him and not to some guy like Cole.

"All you have to do is draw him into conversation," she said.

"And how the fuck am I supposed to do that?" I asked. "You said he was a charming bastard."

"He is," she said. "And his shyness is part of his charm."

"No, it's not," I said. "It's a pain in the ass."

"Kara, listen to me," she said, drawing a breath. "Cole's shy, there's nothing either of us can do about that. I think that's why he's never had an affair, if you want to know the truth. He gets really tongue-tied around pretty women. I mean, he's a barracuda of a salesman, but there's something about women that makes him shy. I guess he's just afraid he's going to make a fool out of himself or something."

"Whatever," I said, getting more and more annoyed.

"But, anyway, after you talk to him for just a few minutes, he'll loosen up and, believe me, he'll be so charming you won't be able to stand it."

"I can't stand him right now," I said.

"Just go back out there, sit down and smile at him," she said. "Then ask him what he does for a living. That will loosen him up. He *loves* to talk about his job. Just do that and he'll open up a little and it'll be fine."

"This is way too much trouble," I hissed.

"Listen," she said. "If you have sex with him, it will be well worth it."

"It better be!" I said.

"Okay," she replied. "I gotta go. I'm almost to the bar."

"What? You're not there yet?"

"I got hung up," she said.

"Doing what?"

"The sale at Macy's," she said.

"You went to Macy's?"

"I had to," she said. "I had to have some bags to prove I was there, don't I?"

I didn't have any bags. Oh, good Lord! This was way too complicated. And I was so going to get busted! I could get a divorce over all this. Neil would think I'd lost my mind. And he'd probably be right.

"Call me back if you can't get him to talk," she said.

"Listen, Lily," I said. "I'm having second thoughts about all this. It's wrong, you know?"

"What's so wrong about it?"

"I don't know," I said, trying to think of something that was wrong with it. "It's bad Karma!"

"No, it's not," she said. "It's one chick doing another chick a solid."

I stared at the phone for a second, thinking *she'd* lost her mind, then got back on and said, "What the fuck does that mean?"

"It means," she said, drawing a breath. "That it's one girl helping another girl out so they both don't go crazy in their marriages. It's a favor. That's all it is. Please don't read anything into it."

"Okay, fine."

"So, are you ready to do this?" she asked.

"I think so."

"Well, get to it then," she told me.

"I will," I grumbled.

"Bye."

"See ya," I said and hung up. Never again was I ever letting anyone talk me into doing anything. I checked myself in the mirror, squared my shoulders then went back out and sat down next to Cole. He muttered something.

"What?" I asked, getting even more irritated at him.

"I saved your seat," he said without looking at me.

Then I felt like such a bitch. He was trying to be nice. But I just couldn't do this. This guy, while he was cute, wasn't worth the trouble. And he was really cute. Lily was a lucky bitch. But then, so was I.

"Thanks," I said. "That was nice of you."

He nodded once.

Now what? Now I was going to finish my beer and I was going to leave and try to forget that this had ever happened. If Lily fucked Neil then I'd just have to deal with it. I hoped to God she didn't fuck him.

I picked up the beer and sipped it, then set it back down, shaking my head. It had gotten warm and tasted like crap.

"What is it?" Cole asked.

"The beer sucks," I said.

"Oh!" he said and motioned to the bartender, then pointed at his beer and held up two fingers. The bartender fished two out of the cooler and placed them in front of us, then popped the caps, poured them into a glass and slid them towards us.

"Is that all?" the bartender asked me.

I stared at him. He was so good looking. Damn! I could do him and forget about everything. That way, if Neil had sex with Lily we'd be even. Sounded like a plan to me. I said as smoothly as I could, "Yeah, that's all. Thanks a lot."

The bartender winked at me again and left. Cole cleared his throat.

I smiled at him, took a sip of beer, then a look around. "Crowded in here, isn't it?"

He nodded. "Yeah, it is."

This was so very awkward. What was I doing? Why was I doing it? Why had I let Lily talk me into it? And how could I get the bartender to fuck me?

"This sounds crazy," Cole said, almost stammering. "But I… I know you. I mean, I don't know you, but I've seen you before."

"You have?" I asked, though I knew what he was talking about. "When?"

"A few weeks ago," he said. "At the Dennis' party?"

I pretended to think about it, then said, "Ummm… I don't remember."

He nodded. "I don't know if you saw me or not."

I shook my head.

"You were talking to my wife that night," he said.

I pretended to be confused. "Your wife?"

He nodded. "About your size? Her name's Lily."

Oh, shit. Now he probably was thinking about her and their marriage and how great it was and what was he doing here talking to this girl—me—and not being at home with his pretty wife? And that meant he wasn't thinking about me. That meant, Lily was going to get to fuck my husband and I wasn't going to get to fuck hers. *Bartender!*

"I don't remember her," I said. "I talked to a lot of people that night. The hostess is an old friend of mine."

"Oh," he said. "I was supposed to meet her tonight, my wife, I mean, but she had to go to some sale."

She's already been, buddy. Wait till you get the bill.

"I don't even know why she wanted to meet," he said. "We see each other at home all the time."

Good grief. We were this close to being busted, Lily and I. But then I realized, he hadn't caught on. He was close, but he wasn't there yet. Then I realized he was a man and that meant nothing a woman ever did made much sense to him, whether it was going to a sale or swapping her husband out for a night. He was just along for the ride and anything she did was okay with him as long as he didn't have to invest much brainpower in it and nothing much was asked of him.

Damn, I'd just hit it. I had this whole thing figured out and figuring it out make it easier on me to go through with it. I mean, why not? I was here, after all. I had gotten dressed up for something.

I said, "Well, maybe she just wanted to get out of the house."

"She gets out all the time," he said, then shook his head. "I'm sorry. I don't need to sit here bitching about my wife."

"You're not bitching," I said and changed the subject. "So, tell me a little about yourself."

"Not much to tell," he said.

"What kind of work do you do?"

"I used to be in sales," he said more confidently. "But I got a promotion recently and now I manage a team, go out into the field, all that. It's not so hard. It's a lot less stressful. I enjoy it."

"Oh, congratulations on your promotion."

"Thanks," he said and smiled. "It's great 'cause now I have plenty of time to do what I like. What do you do?"

"I used to be a social worker," I said.

"Oh, that's great."

"It was great for the first five years," I said. "But then, not so great. Burnout rate is high in that field."

"So what do you do now?" he asked and sipped his beer.

"Nothing," I said. "I'm taking time off."

He considered that, nodding, then said, "That must be nicc."

"It really is," I said. "So, anyway, what's your name?"

"Cole," he said. "What's yours?"

"Kara," I replied and held out my hand.

He smiled a little and shook my hand. "Nice to meet you."

"You too," I said and nodded. That's when I knew this thing might just work. He was starting to open up. It might not be a total loss and if it was, there was always the bartender. I thought about what Lily had said about the size of Cole's dick. I wondered if it were true. I leaned back and took him in. He was big, all over. Why wouldn't his dick be big, too?

"So, what do you do now that you're not working?" he asked.

"Nothing," I said. "Just trying to find myself, all that crap."

"And what have you found so far?"

He was starting to flirt a little, which was a good sign. I smiled and said, "Just that I like not working."

He laughed. "Yeah, that would be nice."

I nodded. "I mean, it's nice. Now I can relax a little and decide what I want to do with the rest of my life."

"What do you think you want to do?"

I smiled at him and said, "This sounds crazy, but I want to study anthropology, get a degree in it, you know? I love that kind of stuff."

"It is interesting."

"It is," I said. "Human evolution and how we're biologically engineered, all of that. I love it. Desmond Morris is my hero."

"Who's he?"

"Oh, he's this great guy who's written books on human evolution and sexuality. It's so interesting."

He nodded. "Sounds like it."

I smiled. "It's just a pipe dream that I have, going back to school."

"I never finished school," he said. "Went to college a couple of years, then straight to work."

"That's nice," I said just as my cell rang. I decided to ignore it, but then Cole gave me a strange look, so picked up. "Hello?"

"Kara? It's Lily."

Oh, shit!

"Listen," she said. "I know this sounds crazy, but I can't pick your husband out! I've been standing here for ten minutes looking like a fool!"

"Uh huh," I said, nodding.

"Tell me what he looks like."

I smiled at Cole and put my hand over the phone and said, "I'm going to have to take this. Would you mind saving my seat?"

"Not at all," he said.

I thanked him and went to the bathroom, where I hissed, "Why are you calling me? I'm sitting here talking to your husband!"

"How's it going?" she asked.

"He's actually pretty nice," I said.

"I told you, he's a cool guy," she said. "Once he gets over that initial shyness, he'll probably talk your ear off."

"Good," I said. "So what do you want?"

"I can't pick Neil out," she said. "All these guys in this bar seem the same. They've all got business suits on."

"Okay, let me think," I said. "He wore a dark pinstriped suit with a yellow tie."

"That just described half the assholes in here!"

"Oh, I know," I said. "He's got these really cool shoes on. They've got a slightly thick sole and are made of this really shiny leather."

"Hold on," she muttered. "Wait a minute. Does he have a pinkie ring?"

"He's not supposed to wear that thing!" I almost yelled. "You'd think he was a fucking gangster!"

"Well, does he or doesn't he have one on?"

"Yeah," I groaned. "And he's also got this scar above his lip. He fell down the stairs once."

"Oh, yeah! That's him!"

"Good," I said and checked my make-up in the mirror.

"He looks good," she said and giggled. "I can't believe I'm doing this!"

"I know!" I squealed. "It's crazy, isn't it?"

"But it's so fun!"

"Yeah, it is," I said.

"Well, let me go," she said. "Wish me luck!"

"Good luck!" I said and hung up. Had I just wished another woman good luck so she could go fuck my husband? Yeah, I had.

As I went back out, I noticed Cole was staring at the TV again. He really liked to watch the game, didn't he? I was so glad Neil had never gotten into that crap. But as soon as he spotted me, he smiled and pushed out the stool for me.

"Saved it for you," he said. "Some guy tried to take it but I told him it was yours."

"Thank you," I said and smiled at him.

"Are you hungry?" he asked.

"Actually, I am," I said.

"I know a good place," he said. "Wanna go grab a bite?"

"Sure."

He paid the tab and we left, but then we had to drive separately to the little restaurant which was almost across town. He hopped out of his sports car and then trotted over and opened my door for me. *How sweet!* I'd forgotten how nice it was for a guy to make a fuss over me.

"You'll love this place," he said. "They've got great burgers."

"I always like a burger," I said.

We went in and were seated and then he started to act a little antsy, squirming in his chair, tapping his foot.

"What's wrong?" I asked.

"You don't think this is weird, do you?" he asked.

"What's weird?" I asked.

"That we're married and having dinner," he said. "It's like I just asked you, you agreed and here we are. It's kind of weird."

It was weird, but then again, the whole situation was weird. I had decided to just go with it. I didn't really expect to fuck him anymore and was actually just enjoying his company. It was so nice to just talk to another person without worrying about what my husband might think. It was so nice just to be me. But wait a minute, how did he know I was married?

"How do you know I'm married?" I asked.

"I saw you at that party with a guy," he said. "I just assumed…"

"Oh," I said and looked down at the menu.

"Well, are you?"

"Married?" I asked. "Yeah, I am."

"Oh, shit," he said. "We shouldn't do this."

"Cole," I said. "All we're doing is having dinner. It's not like we're going to… You know."

He seemed confused, then sighed as if that's what he'd wanted me to say, but was disappointed that I had.

"Yeah," he said quickly. "I know that. I wasn't assuming anything."

"I know you weren't," I said. "Let's just have a little dinner and then we can leave and everything's cool, okay?"

He nodded. "Okay. We can do that."

So we had a little dinner and drank a little, all the while talking. He told me all kinds of stuff about himself and I told him all kinds of stuff about myself. It was so nice. I'd forgotten how nice it was just to talk to someone new. To talk to someone who didn't already know everything about me.

After dinner, he paid the check and we walked out to my car where we stood for a long few seconds. *Awkward! What's next?*

"Wow," he said and pointed. "We're close to the Four Seasons."

I looked up the street and saw the hotel in the distance. "That we are."

He swallowed hard and cleared his throat. I waited. Say it! Say it!

"It's a nice place," he said.

"I've never been in there," I said. "Is it nice?"

"Yeah, it's real nice," he said, then casually, "You wanna go check it out?"

"Sure," I said and teased, "I mean, as long as you promise not to try any funny stuff."

"Oh, I'd never do that," he said nervously.

We'll see about that.

"Then let's go," I said. "You can drive."

"Sure," he said and opened my door.

I grinned at him, got in and realized that, while I was nervous, I was also excited. The great thing was, I was really comfortable with this guy. It was like we already knew each other or something. Well, I knew about him, thanks to his wife.

As we drove up the street, I realized that if I went through with this everything would change. Even if I tried to fool myself into thinking it wouldn't, I knew it would. And if Neil fucked Lily it would change even more.

I almost panicked, almost told Cole to stop the car and let me out. I didn't know if I had the guts to go through with this or not. I didn't know how I'd act. Most importantly, I didn't know who I'd be after we did it. But then again, there is no reward without risk. But then again, if there is no risk, there's no foul.

Cole pulled up to the hotel and said, "Ready?"

I stared at him and realized I was ready. I was ready to see what I'd been missing out on, if anything. I was ready to move on with my life and if that meant it changed, then that's what it meant. Change is always inevitable, right? I was going to do it, no matter what. And I was going to do it because I knew that if I didn't, I wasn't living life the way I wanted to live. And it was about time for a change anyway.

"I'm ready," I told him.

Virgin adulteress.

Once we were in the suite at the hotel, I looked around and realized I was nervous. I was in a hotel room with a strange man! I was about to get some strange! I was about to have sex with a stranger. And that's what he was, a stranger. Even if I knew his wife and even if we'd had a nice conversation and a nice dinner, Cole was still a stranger to me. What the hell had I gotten myself into?

But there was no backing out. This was it. This was my chance to step up and get something I'd wanted for years. This was my chance to see what sex with another man would feel like. This was my chance to savor life.

Oh, shit. I still didn't know how I'd gotten myself into this.

"Nice room, isn't it?" he asked and threw the key down on the coffee table.

I looked around and nodded.

"Would you like a drink?"

“Sure,” I said and watched him prepare us both a drink at the mini-bar. What was I doing? What the hell was I doing? I was about to have sex with someone other than my husband, that’s what I was doing. If I was going to do it, I might as well get started. I didn’t want to drag this out. I wanted to do it, get it over with and then leave.

“Here,” he said and handed me the drink, then clinked his glass to mine.

“Thank you, Cole,” I said and summoned my courage. Then I went to the big bed in the other room and sat down.

He followed me but stopped in the doorway. Then he shifted his feet nervously and stared at a spot on the wall above my head.

Courage, don’t fail me now! I took a breath and tried to sound as sexy as possible, “This is a nice bed, isn’t it?”

He stared at the bed then at me and nodded.

I patted the bed. “Why don’t you take a load off?”

“Don’t mind if I do,” he said and walked over and sat down. “It’s been a long day.”

“That it has,” I said.

We sat there for a long moment, neither of us willing to make the next move. I was almost about ready to change my mind when he muttered something.

“What?” I asked.

He cleared his throat and said, “Are we going to have sex?”

“Where the hell did that come from?” I asked, pretending to be shocked.

“It’s just…” he said. “I don’t know. I’m so nervous I don’t know what I’m doing or saying.”

I smiled gently at him. He was really nervous, even more nervous than me. For a large man, he had a quiet demeanor. He was shy and a little more laid back than most of the men I’d known. That made me think he would be a wild man in bed. You had to watch those quiet ones. When he spoke, he said what he meant; he didn't beat around the bush and he didn't bullshit. And, I'd be willing to bet, when he fucked he fucked good, concentrating on every move with a lot of intensity.

Thinking about him like that turned me on beyond belief. I was going to do him. I was so going to fuck his brains out. Now I was ready, I was ready to get the show on the road.

"I'm nervous, too," I said and laid my hand on top of his. "But we can just talk if you like."

"I don't want to just talk," he muttered. "That's the problem."

I felt my heart begin to pick up its pace.

"I mean," he said quietly, looking into my eyes. "You're so hot."

I felt heat rise in my cheeks as I blushed. I loved hearing stuff like that but then again, what woman doesn't?

"When I saw you that night," he whispered and moved in close to me. "I forgot for a minute that I was married."

Wow.

"You looked so good," he said and pressed his face in my neck. "So good I wanted to fuck you right then and there. I had to leave the room for a minute, if you know what I mean."

Did that mean he got a hard-on just looking at me? Now *that* was a compliment. I was hard-on good! I'd always wanted to be one of those women who drove men crazy, to the point that they couldn't help but make a fool of themselves. Now, maybe, I was one of those women. I liked being that woman.

"Mmm," I moaned and found my hands playing with his hair.

He pulled back. "I don't know, but I was going to talk to you. When I came back into the room, I saw you talking to my wife. I hated that she'd gotten to talk to you and I hadn't. I thought that meant we could never… You know."

I stared into his eyes. "Yeah?"

"Oh, shit," he said and got up off the bed. "What the fuck am I doing?"

I sat up and watched as he began to pace.

"I'm fucking around on my wife!"

I wanted to yell, *And she's fucking around on you! It's really no big deal!* But I didn't. I wanted to, though, so bad. Fucking Lily! She was ruining it all!

"I'm sorry, Kara," he said. "I don't think I can do this."

A loud sigh came out of my mouth, then I rolled my eyes. Men! They never did what you expected of them. From taking out the trash to fucking around, they never did! And she was giving him permission. If I could only tell him that… He'd think we were both insane.

"I'm so sorry," he said and sat down on the bed near me, but not next to me. "I love her."

And she loves you and I love my husband and what's wrong with this picture? I thought I was hard-on good! And I'd just talked myself into it to have him pull the rug out from under me. Fuck!

"Kara," he said and took my hand. "If I wasn't married, I'd fuck you in a second flat."

I couldn't help it. I cracked up. I laughed so hard I was rolling around the bed. He stared at me in disbelief for a moment before he began to laugh, too. Soon, we were both holding our stomachs and shaking our heads. This was too much! It was too crazy. But it had been fun. Something different. And if Lily got to fuck my husband and I didn't get to fuck hers? Well, more power to her. She was a better woman than me and I'd hand it to her.

"What is so funny?" he asked and pushed the hair out of my face.

"Life," I said and took his head between my hands. "Life is so funny, Cole! Isn't it? It's just so fucked up with its rules and regulations."

"Yeah," he said. "It is."

"Ah," I said and shook my head at him. "At least we gave it a try."

"I didn't mean to bring you down with my issues," he said softly.

"That's okay," I said and felt disappointed.

"I really want to, though," he said. "It's just that I've never done anything like this and I don't know how to act."

But he knew how to pay for drinks and dinner and open car doors and save seats and get rooms at the Four Seasons, didn't he? He knew how to act, that wasn't the problem. The problem was he was feeling guilt and it was messing with his perception, just as it had been messing with mine. Didn't we own our bodies? Didn't we feed them and clothe them and take care of them? Why couldn't we do with them what we wanted to do? What was so wrong with me and him having sex anyway? It's not like we were taking something away from our spouses and giving it to someone else, was it? Was sex so sacred that it couldn't be shared? Even when we wanted to share it?

I didn't know. All I knew was that there was nothing I could do about it. He was a hard nut to crack. Lily should have warned me about him.

We sat quietly for a few moments. Then I turned to him and asked, "Do you like being married?"

"Yeah," he said. "I guess I do. Do you?"

I shrugged. "I like it sometimes, but sometimes, I don't like it."

"What would your husband think about you being here with me?"

An image of Neil and Lily fucking raced through my mind. But it didn't upset me. I wanted him to have that, even if I couldn't. And I knew he was dying for it, too. We all are. It's in all of us.

"I don't know what he'd think," I said. "There's this opinion I have of marriage that if something like that happens, it's just best to keep it under your hat. You're only going to hurt the other person by telling them. I mean, don't let your own guilt ruin their lives, you know?"

"That makes a lot of sense," he said.

"I mean," I said. "If he has done something like this, I don't want to know. That's his life, that's his problem. It's like when we get married, we take on all this baggage and we hold each other back from our basic human needs. And let's face it, it's in all of us to cheat."

"So you're saying it's not a bad thing, it's just something that humans do with each other but because we're married, we force ourselves not to do it?"

"And not to think about it," I said. "And to feel guilty if we do. We take something that is so innately human—sexuality—and we turn it into his ugly thing. Here's the kicker—without it, none of us would be around to get mad about it or feel weird about it."

"Wow," he said. "You've got that down."

"That's what I'm going to study someday," I said proudly. "Human sexuality and the evolution of it. I want to know why we're so weird about it, what caused us to make these judgments about it. Why it all got so convoluted in the first place. I mean, did cavemen worry about sleeping around? No! And they didn't because if they did, they wouldn't be able to procreate and get their genes into the next generation."

"You are so smart," he said. "And all this talk is making me hot."

"Is it really?" I asked and leaned back to stare at him.

"I want you," he said. "There's no question of that. It's just I don't want to hurt her."

God, that was so sweet of him.

"But what she doesn't know, can't hurt her," he said. "Can it?"

I grinned. "No, it can't."

"You wanna give it a try?"

"Only if you do," I said. "I mean, I don't want to corrupt you."

He laughed quietly, then said, "I think I would be the one corrupting you."

He didn't know nothing, that was for sure. Besides, I wanted to be corrupted to a certain extent. It was the not knowing what it was like that drove me to these extremes. Not knowing always does us in, though, doesn't it?

"Have you done this before, Kara?" he asked.

I shook my head. "No, I'm a virgin adulteress."

He cracked up. "So that's what it's called?"

"I think so," I said. "I mean, no, I've never cheated but don't think I haven't thought about it. A lot."

"I have too."

"You have?"

He nodded. "It's just nice to know I'm not the only one with thoughts like this."

"Believe me," I said. "You're not."

"That's nice to know."

"It is, isn't it?" I teased and slid over to him. "I promise to be gentle."

"I just want to make sure that you really want to do this."

“I really do, Cole,” I said and moved closer to him on the bed. “I really do.”

He grinned at me as I got on my knees and bent to kiss him. His lips were soft, wet and inviting. I pressed mine against his and once his mouth opened, I felt electricity course through my body. Now this was nice. I’d forgotten how good it felt to kiss someone new. To have a new person’s lips on mine. It was a long damn time ago; too damn long.

Our kiss became fevered and I found my body beginning to press into his. His big hands were in my hair, grabbing onto the back of my head and holding it still as we kissed. It was such a good kiss, too, wet and hot and all tongue and sucking and licking. It was divine but soon, it deepened and we really began to get over our nervousness and concentrate on the kiss. The kiss was leading us to other things. Things that were going to give us an enormous amount of pleasure.

He pushed me back onto the bed and pressed his body into mine. I shivered with delight as he ran his thumb across my lips. He grunted with pleasure as I sucked his thumb into my mouth, staring into his eyes as I did so. He pulled it out and pushed his lips against mine and we kissed again, this time more feverishly, as if something had taken us over and we couldn’t stop doing it.

He settled in and pressed his face into my neck where he began to lick and suck at it. Ahh! *Yes!* It felt so good. I could feel the warmth of his body and the whiskers of his five o’clock shadow scratching my face. He kept at it for a moment before his hand began to unbutton my shirt. I waited with bated breath as he did that, as he fumbled with the buttons and then pushed the shirt open to reveal my breasts, which were heaving in my bra and wanting to be played with.

Without an ounce of the hesitancy he'd shown earlier, he grabbed my breasts and with both hands and squeezed them, then pressed his face into them. I threw my head back and moaned. I moaned even louder when he unsnapped my bra, pulled it off me and grabbed onto a nipple with his mouth as the other hand squeezed my other breast.

Then his hand was going lower and lower. The anticipation of it was driving me mad. His hand slipped under my skirt and then I felt his thumb slipping inside my panties.

"You are so wet," he muttered and kissed at my mouth. "So hot."

"Mmm," I moaned and wanted more. His whole hand was resting flat against my pussy then he began to move it, up and down. I went with his motion and began to grind against it as he kissed his way down my body. I writhed and wriggled as he made his way down. He made it there and in one quick motion, pulled the panties from my body, pushed my skirt up and dove in.

I nearly bucked up from the bed. His mouth was all over my pussy, licking and sucking at it as his fingers explored it and then pushed inside me, into my cunt.

"Oh, yeah," I said and felt the orgasm. Oh, yeah! It was coming at me and it was coming so fast and hard, I lost my breath. It was a good one that made me grind against his face and want more and more.

As it left me and I was still tingling, I grabbed onto his head and pulled him back up to me. I pushed and tugged at his clothes until he was naked and then I grabbed onto his hard and throbbing cock. Lily was right. It was a big one! Jackpot! It was long and thick and looked good enough to eat. I pushed him back on the bed and licked and kissed my way down his body to his dick which was waiting on me, waiting on my mouth.

A hiss came out of his mouth as I took it into my mouth and began to suck on it. I went up and down on it, sucking it with everything I had. I went up and down, deepthroating him a few times, which made him run his hands through my hair, then push it back so he could watch what I was doing.

"You give the best head of anyone I've ever known," he moaned. "Oh, God, don't stop."

I didn't stop. I kept at it and began to play with his balls as I did so, then I licked my way down the shaft and sucked on his balls. He nearly rose up from the bed when I did that. I grinned at him and went back down on it.

"Baby, you're going to have to stop that," he muttered. "Or there'll be nothing left."

I gave the tip one more suck and then nibbled at it, eyeing him as I did so.

"I mean it, come here," he said and grabbed me around the waist and plopped me down in front of him. "I want to fuck you."

That turned me on so much. I grinned and wrapped my arms around his neck and pulled him to me. We kissed as he settled between my legs and then ground into me until his cock just slid on in. I gasped a little. It was that big. Oh...*oh!* Oh, yeah! It was big and it filled me up. I squeezed my pussy around it and he gasped a little and stared into my eyes. I nodded and began to ride him. He rode me, too. Soon, we were slamming into each other, eating at each other's mouths, then he pulled back and ate at my tits.

"Oh, yeah," he moaned and licked at my neck.

I fucked that big dick and before I knew what was happening, I was coming. My arms went over my head and I clawed at the headboard. It was deep, intense orgasm, wrapped up in pure joy and ecstasy. It made me feel every single part of my body, it made me feel alive.

He was coming too. He was coming hard, pumping into me so hard, the whole bed shook with his movements. I held onto him as he came and felt his hot cum shoot inside me. He kept moving inside me for a moment as he came and I moved with him, smiling and feeling… Feeling so refreshed.

"Mmm," he moaned and kissed me. "That was so good."

"It really was, wasn't it?" I said breathlessly.

He leaned back and stared into my eyes. "Wow. You're a good fuck."

I threw my head back and laughed. "Well, thanks, Cole, you're a good fuck, too."

"I mean it," he said. "I haven't had sex like that in… Well, ever."

I stared at him. "You haven't?"

"No," he said. "Have you?"

I thought about it. Neil and I always had good sex, even when we were pissed off at each other. But Cole was right. While I'd had good—excellent even—sex, it had never been like this. Probably because Neil and I were so familiar with each other and when we'd first starting having sex, I wasn't that experienced and didn't know how to do it right. Neil had been a good teacher, though.

"Uh, no," I said. "I don't think I have."

He grinned. "I liked it."

"I'm glad," I said and kissed his cheek, then glanced at my watch. Good Lord! It was almost eleven! I had to get home!

"What's wrong?"

"I have to get home," I said and pushed him off me.

"Me too," he said. "But I want you to know, I'm really glad I met you."

"I'm glad I met you, too," I said and smiled at him. He really was a cool guy. Lily was a very lucky woman. But then again, Neil was great, too. So, I was lucky as well.

We got dressed without talking, then walked to the door, where he stopped and pulled me to him and kissed me again.

"We should do this again," he said, pulling away. "I mean, if you want to."

"I'll see what I can do."

He nodded and then broke out into a big, old happy grin.

"What is it?" I asked.

"It's just," he said. "I'd forgotten how good it feels."

I smiled. Me, too. That was the point of all this.

When I got home, Neil was already in bed. I felt guilt for a second, then climbed in beside him.

He mumbled, "You home?"

"No," I said, then cracked up.

"Good God, Kara!" he hissed. "I have to get up early tomorrow."

I stared at him, wondering how he felt after having sex with a stranger. I wanted to ask him, to find out if he felt happy like I did. But I couldn't bring myself to. But I did hope he felt as good as I did about the whole thing.

Woman on top.

The plan was to meet at our diner, talk about what had conspired and then go our separate ways. Only problem was, I didn't want to go our separate ways. I wanted more of what I had last night. I didn't know if I had the balls to ask for it, though. But damn, it had been so good. I had woken up thinking about it. I was so horny, I had climbed on top of Neil, who asked what the hell I was doing.

"I'm going to fuck you," I said and bent to kiss his lips.

"You are?" he asked and grinned, then pulled my head in closer. "I can handle that."

It was a good fuck, too and early morning fucks were always the best, though we hadn't done that in a while. It's like the skin is just waking up and starting to tingle. You start to feel awake, alive and then the sex just makes you feel better and better. The great thing was that Neil usually woke up with a hard-on anyway. So he was just as ready as I was. All I had to do was climb aboard and move a little. He moved some too. Soon, we were fucking with me, woman on top. One of the best, if not *the* best, positions around.

I began to move on top of him, going up and down on his hard cock, then grinding myself against him. He sat up and grabbed onto my tits and began to suck at my nipples, which just sprang to attention. Ah, that felt so good.

It didn't take long before we were fucking like crazy, shaking the bed. The orgasm, for both of us, was quick and delightful. When it was over, we kissed a little and eyed each other slyly.

It hadn't been that good in a long damn time. But that's not why were giving each other the sly looks. We were giving each other the sly looks because we both knew what was up and why we were so turned on. Not that we'd say anything and why should we? That would just ruin both of our days.

The added bonus was that he was so happy he'd gotten laid, he didn't ask me any questions about last night. He didn't even want to know what time I'd gotten home. And I didn't ask him anything, either.

And he even kissed me before he left to go to work! He never did stuff like that anymore. Maybe this hadn't been a bad idea. It was almost as if we appreciated each other or something.

But now, I had to confront Lily. As I approached the diner door, I began to feel a little apprehension. How did she feel? Did she have a good time? Was she pissed off at me for fucking her husband? Well, I wasn't pissed off at her for fucking mine. In fact, I was about ready to kiss her for it. Maybe she wouldn't be pissed off at me. And if she was? Tough shit. Nothing was going to ruin my day today. I was in too good of a mood for that.

Lily was waiting on me in a booth in the back of the dinner. She smiled when she saw me and as soon as I sat down, she said, "How are you?"

I smiled back and said, "I haven't felt this good in years."

"Me either!" she squealed. "So did you do it?"

I nodded. Just then Dena, the waitress from before, came up and slid two glasses of tea on the table.

"So, ladies," she said. "The usual?"

We smiled at her and nodded. She winked and left.

"So tell me what happened," Lily whispered, excitedly.

I hesitated and said, "I'm afraid if I tell you what happened, you'll get pissed."

"Well," she said. "Tell me anyway."

"Why?"

"I don't know! Just do!"

"Okay, but don't get pissed," I said.

"I won't," she said. "Tell me."

"So, anyway, we met and then…" I paused, considering my words. "He was very nervous."

"He couldn't get it up," she muttered. "I knew it!"

I stared at her in disbelief. "No, he got it up and it stayed up, that wasn't the problem."

"Then what was the problem?"

"At first he didn't want to do it," I said. "Because of you."

"Neil did that too."

"Really?" I asked. "How sweet!"

"Well, I thought it was annoying," she said.

"I guess it was a little annoying, now that you mention it," I said. "But anyway, we talked some and I guess he got comfortable."

Her eyes narrowed at me. "So he did fuck you?"

"Yeah, I told you he did," I said and almost blushed. "He's really good, too."

She nodded. "I know."

"So, how was mine?" I asked.

"Well," she began. "First of all, just let me say, he's a great kisser."

"Uh huh."

"But we didn't have sex," she said.

I hated to admit, but I got some satisfaction from that. "Why not?" I asked, pretending to be shocked.

"We just talked."

"About what?" I asked.

"You know," she replied, looking around the restaurant. "About life and stuff."

"You didn't do anything?"

"Oh, we fooled around."

"What did you do?" I asked.

"What do you mean?"

"I mean, did you kiss, did you have oral sex... That kind of stuff. What did you do?"

"We just made out," she said.

"Why didn't you have sex?"

"He said that he wasn't sure I knew what I was doing," she said. "And he wanted to make sure so I wouldn't look back on this and regret it."

"It's just sex!" I almost shouted. "What is he? Some chivalrous bastard all of a sudden?"

"He must be," she said. "It's weird that he's like that and you didn't know."

I tried to not let that bother me and said, "Yeah, that is weird."

She nodded just as Dena slid our plates of food onto the table.

"So," Dena said. "Anything changed since we last talked?"

We grinned at her and nodded.

"And was it everything you'd hoped?"

We glanced at each other and nodded.

"No going back, ladies," she said. "Let me know if you need anything else."

I watched her leave, then turned to Lily.

"What is it?" she asked and sipped her tea.

I hesitated, but then blurted, "So, anyway, can we do it again?"

She cracked up and said, "I thought you'd never ask."

"Good," I said.

"You know," she told me. "I think it's not just the sex I was after."

My ears pricked up. "What do you mean?"

"I mean," she said and picked up her burger. "I liked just talking to him, you know?"

"Wow," I said. "I liked that too. But the sex was really good."

"Yeah," she said and took a small bite.

"So, are you going to do it with him the next time?" I asked.

"Oh, yeah," she said offhandedly. "I wanted to last night but he said we should wait and that I might change my mind and all that."

I nodded.

"He's a really cool guy, that husband of yours."

"He is," I said. "But your husband is cool too."

"I know," she said. "I guess I just don't appreciate that part of him anymore."

"So, does this mean…? You know, that we can do it again?"

She nodded eagerly. "Let's not give it up just yet! I mean, I still have to get mine, you know? So, you're welcome to my husband for a little bit longer. I mean, as long as I'm welcome to yours."

I nodded and grinned at her. Then we stared at each other than cracked up. I was laughing so hard tears were rolling down my cheeks. It was so good to laugh like this again. And we kept laughing and kept talking until lunchtime was over and it was time to leave.

"You know," Lily said and smiled at me. "I am so glad I took a chance with you."

"I'm glad you did too," I said. And I was. I was so glad we'd met and been able to make this thing work. I was so glad I'd taken a chance. Life could be so good sometimes. And now I had something to look forward to. I had a fuck buddy.

As I left the diner, I could have thrown my hat into the air and twirled around. Too bad I wasn't wearing one.

Too damn good.

Cole and I were both so turned on, we just jumped at each other. We didn't look around the hotel room or ask how our days had been. He grabbed me, threw me down on the bed and started tearing my clothes off. I tore his clothes off, too, until we were both naked and rolling around the bed.

"I just want to eat you," he moaned as he settled between my legs. "Ummm…"

Yeah, ummm. He pushed his face in there and breathed in. Ahh! Yeah, baby. He began to eat at me, like he was licking an ice cream cone. It felt so good; it felt almost too good and a hiss came out of my mouth. I felt his fingers then, exploring my pussy, making it even wetter than it already was. He stroked my clit until it throbbed. Another hiss came out of my mouth and I had suck my lips into my mouth to keep from crying out with pleasure.

Then he did something different. He pushed a finger inside and then he moved it, like he was rubbing something. Oh, good God! He'd hit my g-spot! I never thought much about it before, but it was there and he was playing with it, rubbing it gently as his mouth sucked at everything else.

He rose up and watched my face as he fingered me. I stared down at him and couldn't do anything but watch his face, watching me. Before I could stop myself, I was coming. It was a different kind of orgasm, too, one I'd never felt before. It was like all the blood in my body was being drained ounce by ounce then being replaced with fire. Every cell in my body woke up and began to pulsate. I was pulsating. It felt dirty, good dirty and it felt fine. It was almost like I had a sudden urge to pee. Then I knew what it was. It was an ejaculation. I had heard about females doing this but I didn't think it was true. But it was true because before I knew what I was doing, I was squirting; I was having a female ejaculation.

It was so hot. I was boiling hot. I was so turned on and so overheated, I was about to explode. A scream tore out of my throat. I couldn't stop it, either. It just came out as I came. My body shook and I grabbed onto him and pulled him to me, wrapping my legs around his waist, wanting to have him on me, in me, fucking me. But then it died down and I just lay there panting. I couldn't speak. I was, for the first time in my life, speechless.

I'd never done that before. Never. I stared at him in disbelief. He'd made me come like that? How did he do that? Could he do it again?

"I can't believe that," he muttered. "You just did that!"

I stared at him and nodded.

He grinned at me and said, "I've never seen a chick do that before."

I grinned back. "Thank you for doing it to me."

"I want to do it again," he said. "You are so hot."

"Wait," I said. "Come here."

We kissed, sucking at each other's mouths. *Ummm.* I felt so alive and ready. I felt so good. Why hadn't I been doing this before now? Who wouldn't want to feel this good? Who wouldn't want to do this all the time? It was better than anything in the world.

I pushed him back and said, "Now it's your turn."

I kissed my way down his body and to his dick, took it in my mouth and began to suck on it. I was so turned on, I wanted to suck him dry. I kept at it, licking up and down and then concentrating on the tip. He lay there and panted as I sucked him off.

"Oh, baby," he moaned. "You do that so good."

I grinned and really went at it then. I loved knowing he loved what I was doing, that it gave him so much pleasure. He couldn't contain himself. His hands were in my hair, pulling it a little as I gave his cock a good going over. He watched my face, my mouth as I sucked on him, then threw his head back and grunted.

And then, he was pumping into my mouth. He kept pumping and I kept sucking, holding his dick as I sucked and then I tasted his cum. That turned me on even more and I sucked harder, stroking his balls as I did so. He erupted into my mouth with all his hot white cum. I couldn't help it, I swallowed and wanted more. I sucked him dry and until there was nothing left.

He fell back on the bed and breathed heavily. I gave his cock one last suck, then rubbed my face into his stomach, then up to his chest then to his neck, where I breathed in his smell.

"Wow," he muttered.

Yeah, wow. That was another thing I had never done before. I'd never swallowed before. Wow. I smacked my lips. It actually didn't taste that bad and I'd heard it was great for your complexion. He stared at me, his eyes wide and sexy. I bit my bottom lip and stared back. He chuckled and kissed me. I kissed back and climbed onto his chest and rubbed against it. He held my hips still and stared into my eyes.

"You are so…" he said, then stopped. "You're just too damn good."

He was right. And I was getting better. I was getting everything I'd always wanted and it made me better.

I grinned at him and said, "Flattery will get you everywhere."

He chuckled and said, "I'm not just blowing smoke up your ass. I really mean it. You're damn good."

"Thanks."

"Tell me some more of that stuff you were talking about the other day."

"What?" I asked.

"You know, about the human evolution or whatever it was."

"Oh," I said and grinned. "Let's see… I just think it's funny how people get so bent out of shape about sex. Forget world hunger! Let's get pissed off about sex!"

He chuckled and said, "Go on."

"I just think people should grow up," I continued. "They keep themselves at this very immature level and over what? An orgasm here or there?"

"Some people might say that you're trying to justify cheating."

I stared at him from the corner of my eye. "Why do you have to justify it at all?"

"You don't," he said. "I get it. I get that it's in all of us because if it wasn't, why would it feel so good? I mean, we were meant to do it. If not, we wouldn't all be worried about it all the time."

I nodded, moved over and grabbed his cigarettes off the nightstand "It's like sex is everywhere. It's in everything we do, how we behave. There's no outrunning it and why would you want to in the first place? Without it, we wouldn't be talking to each other right now."

He nodded and gave me slight smile that made my heart warm.

"Besides," I said, lighting a cigarette. "Putting down sex is stupid because it's the very thing that put your ass here on earth in the first place."

He cracked up and said, "Yeah, that's true."

"I dunno," I sad and puffed on the cigarette. "But I've always been passionate about this subject. I don't want to bore you with it."

"You're not boring me."

I smiled at him. "Good."

"Next time we meet," he said and then grew a little embarrassed. "Could you, uh, dress up?"

I raised an eyebrow. "Dress up?"

He looked down, then back up at me and said, "Like a schoolmistress with glasses and everything?"

"Really?" I asked and leaned back to stare at him. "You want me to do that?"

He nodded eagerly. "I want you to teach me everything you know."

I threw my head back and laughed loudly. "I think I can do that."

He grinned and took the cigarette out of my hand and smoked it. "Thanks."

"So is that your fantasy?"

"One of them."

"Really?" I asked.

"Yeah, really," he said and handed the cigarette back. "What do you see yourself doing in the future?"

I thought about it. "I'll be honest. I'd love to travel, see different cultures, spend some time in Europe."

"I'd like to do that, too."

"Wouldn't it be fun?" I asked. "Of course, there's the language barrier but I think I could get by. I'm awfully charming."

"That you are," he said and chuckled at my facetiousness. "What else do you see yourself doing?"

I shrugged and smoked. "I dunno. I've always been so concentrated on other things, I've never really given what I wanted to do much thought. Just trying to get things done doesn't leave much time for fantasizing."

"But you'd like to travel?"

"Most definitely," I said. "And you, too?"

He nodded. "I'd like it. I'd like to just pack my bags, quit my job and go somewhere."

"I've thought about doing that, too!"

"But you can't," he said. "Responsibility.

"Yeah," I said. "Responsibility sure does suck."

He stared at me.

"What?" I asked.

"Nothing," he said. "But I have to say, I really, really like you, Kara. You've got a way with words."

I laughed and said, "And a dirty mind."

"That's the best part about you."

Yeah. It was good.

• • •

Lily's mouth dropped open. "*No!*"

I nodded.

"You did?"

"I did. He did something with his fingers and I was so turned on, I just felt like...peeing but it wasn't pee, it was the other stuff."

She just stared at me. "He never did that for me."

I shrugged. "It's weird, isn't it?"

She nodded. "It is weird."

"But anyway," I said. "Did you fuck Neil?"

She blushed. She actually blushed!

"You did!" I squealed. "How was it?"

She smiled and sighed, "That man knows his way around a woman."

"I taught him well," I said.

"He just... He took his time and he was so very intuitive about the whole thing. It seemed like we did it for hours."

I nodded. "He's good."

"He really is," she said. "I couldn't have picked a better man to do it with than him."

"Me either," I said and thought about something, then blushed.

"What are you blushing for?"

"Nothing," I said. "It's just after I did that thing, I... Oh, forget it!"

"No," she said. "Tell me."

"I swallowed," I said and stared her head in the eye.

"Swallowed what?"

"Him," I said. "His cum."

"Oh," she said. "So?"

"I've never done that, not even with my husband."

"Really?" she asked, surprised, scrunching up her face.

"Really," I said. "But I liked it."

She nodded. "Good."

Yeah, good. Too damn good. As we left the diner and parted ways, I couldn't help but smile to myself with a sense of satisfaction. I knew that having sex with another man would bring me joy, but I had no idea how much. And the kicker was, I felt okay doing it because Neil was doing it, too. And what's good for the goose was always good for the gander.

Because I was in such a good mood, I went home and made chili, Neil's favorite dish. Why chili was his favorite dish was anybody's guess, but he loved it and would beg me to make it at least two or three times a month. I would give in twice a month but no more than that. As I made it, I hummed and smiled with satisfaction to myself, thinking about what I was doing, what I was going to do and how much fun I was having doing it.

I put the chili on to simmer and was putting the dishes up out of the dishwasher when he came into the kitchen smiling. He stopped short when he saw me.

"What is it?" I asked.

"Nothing," he said. "I just thought you were out."

"No," I said. "Hey, did you pick up your shirts at the cleaners?"

"Oh, I forgot," he said. "I can go out later and get them, though."

"That's okay, I'll get them tomorrow," I said. "Where have you been?"

"At the gym."

"Oh," I said and closed the dishwasher door.

He sniffed and walked over to the stove. "What are you making?"

"Chili," I said and smiled at him.

He eyed it. "Oh, I don't want any."

My mouth fell. "You don't want any? It's your favorite!"

He shook his head. Then I got it. He didn't want to risk being gassy in case he met up with Lily. Smart man. I didn't want to risk it either.

I leaned across the stove and turned the eye off and said, "We can save it for later, then."

I swear he breathed a sigh of relief.

I turned around to him and said, "So if you don't want chili, what do you want for supper?"

He stared at me and said, "You."

"What the fuck?" I asked and shook my head him.

"You look so hot."

I looked down at my shorts and t-shirt, then back at him. "If you say so."

"I'm so horny for you," he said and stepped to me. "I've been thinking about you all day."

"You have?" I asked.

"Yeah," he said and bent to kiss me. "All day long."

"Oh, okay," I said and wrapped my arms around his neck and pulled him to me. He moaned as soon as my mouth opened and pushed his tongue inside. I sucked on it, then pushed mine inside his mouth so he could do the same thing. We kissed for a moment, then his hand went down my shorts and felt my pussy.

"You're already wet."

I nodded. I was. As I'd been doing housework, I'd started fantasizing bout Cole and got so worked up, I had to get my vibrator and masturbate. I didn't tell him that, though.

He bent down and pulled my shorts off, then licked and sucked at my pussy until I almost came. Then he turned me around, got behind me, unzipped his pants and stuck it in. I gasped with pleasure. That felt so good! He rode me, holding onto my shoulders as he pumped into me. I went with him and we began to fuck hard.

"Oh, baby," he moaned, "You are so tight and wet."

"Mmm," I moaned and put my hand on my clit ad rubbed it. "Yeah! Fuck me hard!"

He fucked me hard. I gasped from the pressure. He kept at it, then his movements became more concentrated which meant he was about to come. Which meant, I was already on my way. The orgasm was a breath away and all I had to do was…nothing. It just came at me. I didn't have to work for it. It just walked right up and smiled. I smiled back at it and threw my head back as it hit, moaning so loud that Neil began to moan with me. We kept moaning until we were spent and panting.

It hadn't been that good in months, maybe even years.

He fell on top of me and caught his breath and said, "Phew! Now that was some good fucking."

He suddenly shivered and shook himself.

I cracked up and shook my head at him.

"What is it?" he asked.

"You're just so… I don't… Sexy!"

"You are too," he said and kissed me. "You're the sexiest woman alive."

He never said stuff like that! Never! I smiled and couldn't help but think that last time this month, we'd had an argument so fierce I'd told him I hated his guts. Funny how an affair can make a person really appreciate their spouse.

Fundamentally promiscuous.

"The female of the species," I said and paced in front of Cole in my school mistress outfit. "Is fundamentally promiscuous."

He nodded eagerly and his eyes took me in, going all over my body. We'd been doing this for a few months now. I'd dress up and he'd get a lecture. It was fun and I loved thinking I was in control, even though I knew as soon as he made a move, he'd be the one calling the shots.

"But, the female is not any more promiscuous than the male."

"Oh, yeah, baby!"

I almost cracked up, then regained my composure. "This is why it is inherently difficult for the species to sustain monogamy. Scientists once believed there was a rare species of birds who were monogamous. But after much study they came to the conclusion that, no, they weren't monogamous, after all."

He grinned at me and winked.

I pointed my finger at him. "Mr. Graves, do you find this lecture humorous?"

"Uh, no ma'am."

"Then why don't you tell the class your take on this tantalizing subject?"

He shrugged and looked around the room. "I just like listening to you, Kara. I don't have to participate."

"Very well," I said and continued pacing. "The sanctity of marriage—the marital institute… What can we say about that? Well, for one thing, do you know where they send criminals? Institutions."

He cracked up, then quieted down. "You know, that still doesn't stop me from wanting to marry you."

"Cole!"

"I know! I'm crazy! But, God, Kara, I love you."

"Cole!" I squealed and nearly fell over. He loved me? Oh, good God. This was getting a little heavy. Lily would be so pissed off if she knew. I made a mental note to never tell her.

"So what?" he said and got out of bed and came to me. "I do. I love you. I hate myself for it, too."

"Well, that's nice," I said dryly.

"No, it's just I have a wife and you have a husband and it's complicated."

"I know, baby," I said. "Believe me, I know."

"God!" he said, throwing his hands into the air. "Before I met you I didn't feel this way."

"What way do you feel?"

"Great," he said." And I feel like shit about it, too."

"Why?" I asked, a little indignantly.

"Because of my wife."

Oh, that. Yeah.

"I mean it's wrong what we're doing," he said, shaking his head with irritation. "But it feels so right and so good. I just wish…"

"You wish what?"

He stared at me. "That it wasn't so complicated."

"Me too."

"I can't remember ever being this happy, Kara," he said. "And I love my wife. I think she's fantastic. But with you, it's different."

"Cole," I said. "That's because we're not married and we don't have the chance to get on each other's nerves. If we were married, you might feel the same way about me as you do about her."

"No, I don't think so," he said. "She bosses me around too much."

I didn't tell him I bossed Neil around a lot, too. Let him think what he wanted to.

"If I wasn't already married," he said. "I'd ask you to marry me."

I almost fell over. Wow. I mean, wow! That was pretty cool.

"You know?" he said expectantly.

I smiled gently at him and told him what I knew he wanted to hear, "And if I wasn't already married, I'd marry you."

"You would?" he asked, as if surprised.

"In a heartbeat," I said, though I wasn't so sure. If I ever got divorced, I didn't know if I'd ever remarry. Marriage wasn't that great, to be honest. It was lot of "Where have you been?" and "Where are you going?" and "What are you doing?" And don't even get me started on the monogamy issues. Or the monotony for that matter.

"Thanks," he said. "I mean it, thanks for saying that."

"You're welcome," I said and resumed pacing, ready to put an end to this slightly depressing subject. "Now where was I?"

"You were about to come over here and sit on my lap, beautiful."

"Now, now," I said. "You haven't learned your lesson for today."

"I know enough, baby," he said. "Come over here and let me show you how much I love you."

I grinned. I liked the way he said that.

"Come on now," he said. "I'm ready to give it to you. You ready to take it?"

"Oh, yes, Mr. Graves," I said and walked over to him. "I was about to sit down on your hard cock and fuck your brains out."

He laughed and nodded. "Climb on board."

I climbed on board. I sat down on top of his cock and settled in his lap, wrapping my arms around his neck.

"I love it that you're not wearing panties under that skirt," he said and sucked at my neck.

"I love your hard cock," I said.

"And I love you," he moaned. "Tell me you love me, too."

I pulled back and stared into his yes, feeling so alive yet at the same time, like I was betraying Neil. And I was betraying him, just as he was betraying me. But why look at it as betrayal when it was just a natural human instinct? Why make it ugly when it was in actuality something very beautiful, something two people were sharing, this kind of love?

"I love you, too, Cole," I said.

He grinned. He liked that. I could tell because he started pumping into me. I rode him and we began to fuck, he began to suck at my breast and soon we were both coming, holding onto each other so tightly.

"Ahh," I moaned as I began to shake with the orgasm. "Oh, baby, baby!"

It left us and we stayed like that, holding each other, for a very long time. I could feel his heartbeat next to mine. I moved so I was even closer to him.

"One day," he said. "We're going to have to make some decisions."

"Please don't," I begged. "Please don't start."

"We are," he said. "And I'm about ready, too."

No matter what happens.

It went on like that for months. I don't know how many because I lost count. All I knew was that I was having the time of my life. Cole would call in the early afternoon and we'd set up our plans to meet later. On my way to meet him, I'd call Neil on my cell and ask him how his day was. He'd inevitably say, "It's going good, but I think I might have to work late." Which meant, he wasn't working late at all. He was going to meet Lily. This was A-OK with me. I'd say that was fine and I'd see him later. All the while, our married sex life got hotter.

One night, I'd just barely made it home before him. It was going on midnight and I'd raced to the shower and was just getting out when I heard his car. I dashed into bed and pretended to be asleep when he came home. Then he got into the shower and I breathed a sigh of relief and lay there staring at the ceiling, trying to remember why I was once so unhappy. I couldn't fathom that now, unhappiness. Years and years of it, of being sexually frustrated, of feeling like there was something wrong with me for wanting sex with other men. Years of feeling crazy, of driving myself crazy, of over-thinking everything, of over-analyzing everything and for what? For nothing.

I was so glad I'd met Lily. She should be commended for the plan she had the balls to come up with. I was going to buy her a really nice gift when I saw her later in the week. We still met once a week, discussed what was going on and any problems we were having. Like, for example, in the beginning, Neil was being cheap and taking her to sleaze bag hotels. She bitched, "I mean, my God! You're not that poor, are you? It's like we're flopping or something!"

"No," I said. "But he can be cheap."

So later that night, at home, I casually mentioned to him someone I "knew" who was having an affair and said, "And the guy takes her to these ratholes! She's thinking about telling him to stick it."

After that, problem fixed. The funny part was, he didn't even catch or was even curious to know which "friend" I was talking about. That's because he didn't want to get caught and he didn't want to stop doing it. He knew it was better not to dwell on the subject too much.

As I lay there, I heard Neil get out of the shower and squeezed my eyes shut. For some reason, I started to giggle and had to push my face into my pillow. This was ludicrous! It was ridiculous! It was so much fun and that's why I was laughing.

He came into the room, stopped at the bed and said, "Kara, are you awake?"

I jerked like he'd woke me up and said, "What is it?!"

"Nothing," he said. "I thought I heard you laughing."

"Fuck, Neil," I groaned. "You woke me up."

"Sounded like you were having a good dream," he said and slid into bed.

If he only knew…

"Night, baby," he muttered and kissed my cheek. "Love you."

"Love you too," I said and sighed.

He pressed his face next to mine and kept it there for a few seconds. What was he doing? He was feeling me up. His hands were all over my body, squeezing here and there and then going between my legs.

"What are you doing?" I asked. "I was asleep."

"Wake up, then."

"Neil," I groaned. "Stop it."

"No," he said and climbed on top of me. "I've been so horny for you all day."

"Really?" I asked.

He nodded and pressed his lips to mine. I moaned with delight. He was a really good kisser. He took his time to taste and to tantalize. Cole just went right at it, sucking and pushing his tongue in. He was a good kisser too, but not as romantic as Neil. I didn't know which one I liked better. They were both pretty damn good at it.

He moved down my body, kissing it and caressing it. He was a good lover, gentle when he needed to be and forceful when it was time. He took his time. Cole was more excitable and sometimes would tear my clothes off as soon as we saw each other. But that was probably because we were new lovers and he wanted to get right to it.

I froze. What was I doing? Comparing my husband and my lover while my husband was making love to me? I shook myself and those thoughts out of my mind and concentrated on Neil. He pushed my legs open and slid his hand in sideways. I moaned and ground against his hand. He smiled at me and I smiled back. It was always so comfortable between us. No nervousness. Just easy.

"Always so wet and ready," he moaned and bent down and licked at my pussy.

Cole had said the same thing.

"Mmm," he moaned and got into it.

I wanted him in me, fucking me. I tugged at him but he refused to stop licking me. I moaned, "Come on and fuck me."

"I can't get enough of it," he said and kept at it.

Well, if he insisted. I lay there and loved the way it felt to have his face between my legs, giving me pleasure and before I knew what I was doing, I was coming. It was a quick one, hard hitting and good. I shivered with it and ground against his face until I was completely and totally finished.

"Now come on," I moaned. "Give me some more."

He came on and stuck his hard cock into me. I smiled with satisfaction but then thought about Cole's dick, how it was a little bigger than Neil's. *Stop it!*

I stopped it and we began to fuck, really getting into it. All of a sudden, I couldn't get enough and I wanted him to drive it in harder. He did and we were bucking up off the bed in our lust and passion for one another. And, I swear, the orgasm was almost simultaneous. It just happened so quick. We were so turned on that it was like just *there* and we took it.

I couldn't ever remember it being that good.

"Ahh!" he moaned. "Oh, baby!"

"Oh, yeah!" I moaned back and held him tight as the orgasm subsided.

We lay there for a moment and reflected. He turned to stare at me and smiled.

"I love you," he said. "You know that, right?"

"And I love you," I said.

"I always will," he said. "No matter what happens, I'll always love you."

No matter what happens... What the hell was he getting at?

"I just want you to know that," he said and hugged me, putting his head on my chest.

"Okay," I said, feeling a little uneasy. But then, I let it go. Life was too short to over-think every single thing. I was done with that part of my life. From now on, I was going on gut instinct and feeling. But I knew my guy was telling me something was wrong.

I decided to ignore it.

The next morning, which was a Saturday, we both got up with smiles on our faces. Then he went downstairs and fixed breakfast! He never did stuff like that. Not that I was complaining...

As we were eating, I started studying a school catalogue. I had decided to go back and get another degree in anthropology. Neil sat across from me at the kitchen table and ate as I poured over the catalogue.

"You look beautiful," he said.

"What?" I asked, not paying attention. "I don't know what classes to take."

"Are you really going back to school?"

"I really am," I said. "I wish I hadn't let my mother talk me into switching majors. I could be done with all this. But she'd rather I be a social worker than an archeologist or even a professor of archeology."

"Well, you know how she is," he said, then his head jerked up like what I had said had just sunk in. "You want to be an archeologist?"

"I've always loved it," I told him. "You know that."

"You never told me."

I stared at him and realized I hadn't. I might have hinted at it, but I never came out and said it. I had said it to Cole, though and Cole had told me I'd make the best archeologist around, even if was just "digging in the ground".

"Well, I meant to tell you," I said and shut the catalogue. "I'll probably go a few months and quit anyway."

He stared at me, shook his head once, then looked down at his plate.

"What is it?" I asked.

"Nothing."

"Oh, come on," I said. "I know something is bothering you, so spill it."

"It's just," he said. "I thought once you quit work, we'd start on the kid thing."

Oh, shit, here it was again.

"I mean," he said. "You promised to think about it."

I nodded. I had promised. The only problem I had was that I'd been in service to children and families for over nine years and that kind of smashed my biological clock. There were always problems to deal with and kids getting abused and all that. My former job had been so much worry and angst that the thought of coming home and taking care of a child had made me nauseous. I should have quit that job years ago before it had taken such a toll on me.

"Just give me a little time, Neil," I said. "You know my old job really did me in on the kid thing."

He nodded. "I know. It's just… Nevermind."

"Just what?" I asked.

"I know this girl who's about your age," he said. "And she really wants kids."

My eyes narrowed because I knew the girl he was referring to. "And?"

"And nothing," he said. "I mean, at your age, it's time to think about it and do something about it. You can't stay young forever."

"You son of a bitch!" I spat. "You know what I've been through and here you are trying to tell me how to feel."

"I'm not trying to tell you anything," he said. "I just think we should have a kid."

I glared at him.

He softened and said, "I'm sorry. It's your decision."

"Damn right it is," I said. "After all, I'll be the one carrying around the baby for nine months and taking care of it for the rest of my life."

"I'll be here, too," he said.

"But it's still a woman's responsibility," I said.

"I know," he said and pushed back from the table. "I know, Kara, I know that. You'd think you were afraid I was going to run out on you or something. I'd think you'd trust me more than that, especially after all this time we've been together."

I watched in dismay as he threw his dishes in the sink and then stomped out of the room. His biological clock was wailing. Oh, yeah, men had them too and sometimes they were stronger than a woman's. At least in this case. And I just felt at a loss to do anything about it.

Lipstick on his collar.

As soon as Lily sat down at our booth the next day, I hissed, "What the hell are you doing to my husband?"

"What the hell are you talking about?" she hissed back and threw her purse down.

"You're not only fucking him," I said. "You're mind-fucking him."

"I beg your pardon?"

I nodded at her. "I know all about it, lady and I am here to tell you to stop."

She crossed her arms and said, "Stop what, Kara?"

"Stop mind-fucking him," I snapped.

"I'm not mind-fucking him!" she snapped back.

"Oh, yeah, you are," I said and leaned across the table. "All he talks about now is having a baby. And I happen to know who put these little thoughts in his head."

"Oh, is that right?" she snapped. "Well, let me ask you what you're doing to my husband. That bastard is talking about quitting his job to 'travel'."

I blanched. Yeah, I'd brought that up to Cole, telling him how wonderful I thought it would be to ditch everything and run around the world for a few years. To see the sights and experience other cultures. We'd discussed going to Thailand, maybe India, but most definitely France. I had to see Paris at least once. But wouldn't it be nice to go all over the world, doing all kinds of things? Wouldn't that be great to just jump up and leave? He'd been very intrigued when I'd said it but I never thought he really wanted to do it. I just thought he was going along with it to please me.

And so I'd fuck him more. Guys were always willing to agree to anything with the promise of getting into a girl's panties.

But seriously. He'd been talking about it with Lily? I glanced at her. Not such a good idea, Cole.

"Let me tell you one thing, Kara," she said. "If he quits his job, I'll divorce him."

My ears pricked up. That's the first time she'd ever mentioned divorce. And the first time I'd thought about it since this whole thing started.

"The man's worked his whole life," I said. "He deserves a break."

"No, he doesn't," she hissed. "I didn't slave for years so he could go off gallivanting around the world. I did not sacrifice to get what I've got to see it go to pot. I didn't do the things I did so he could piss it all away."

"That's a little overdramatic, don't you think?" I asked.

"Hell no, it isn't," she said, shaking her head. "Cole needs to work, Kara. He makes good money but if he takes time off, his career will go down the tubes and I don't want to go back to work just yet. Besides, if he isn't working, he goes crazy, even on the weekends. And when he goes crazy he drives me crazy. He always has to be doing something."

Well, he'd been doing me, so I guess she was right.

"I can't let him even entertain the idea," she said. "Sorry, call me a bitch, but I can't do it. I want to start having kids someday, too and if he quits his job, say goodbye to that."

"I don't think you appreciate him," I said and crossed my arms.

"Like hell I don't," she snapped. "I appreciate that son of a bitch more than anyone else ever could!"

I just stared at her.

"You don't appreciate Neil."

I could have slapped her. Instead I hissed, "Like hell I don't!"

"Oh, please," she said. "If you appreciated him so much, why did you agree to let him fuck me?"

"Cause you talked me into it, you bitch!" I seethed.

She started, then shook her head. "That's not what I meant."

"Then what did you mean?"

"Nothing," she said.

"That's what I thought," I said, nodding at her. We sat there for a long moment in silence, sizing each other up.

"Oh, and by the way," she said, breaking the silence. "Tell Cole to stop sending you roses every time you fuck, okay? It's getting a bit pricey."

Her eyes flashed at me almost viciously and I suddenly felt like crap about the whole thing. Oh, God, we were really fighting, weren't we? I shrunk back into the seat and wished I could disappear. We'd never fought but now we were drawing our battle lines. Why were we suddenly fighting? I didn't know, but I sure as hell wasn't going to let her have the last word.

I rolled my eyes. "Well, then, you tell Neil to stop coming home so late. It's getting awkward and his excuses are getting lamer and lamer. A damn fool would know what he's up to and I'm not going to confront him! I won't do it!"

I noticed other customers staring at us but I ignored them. I didn't care if I was being loud. I was going to make sure she got my point.

"Oh, please," she said. "You stay out all night with Cole."

"At least I don't get lipstick on his collar," I said.

"Can I help it if I don't have nice red lips like yours?" she spat. "Some of us need lipstick!"

"What the fuck does that mean?" I hissed.

"It means that…" She stopped and threw her hands up. "I don't know what it means. Besides, what's the big deal about a little lipstick?"

"I'm just getting sick of cleaning it out of his shirts!" I spat. "And he doesn't even bother to try to clean them himself anymore. I think he wants me to confront him and I'll tell you one damn thing, I ain't doing it!"

"Well, maybe you should," she said.

"What the hell does that mean?" I asked, aghast.

"It means maybe he wants to get caught."

I stared at her, then realized she was right. The bastard wanted to be found out. Oh, and then what? I thought about it. Oh. Ohhh, no!

"Sorry," she muttered under her breath, then her face softened and then she said, "Oh, shit."

"What?" I growled.

"Oh, shit, shit, shit!"

"What is it?" I almost yelled.

She stared me dead in the eye and said, "Kara, don't you see what's happening? We're falling for them! They're bringing out the best in each of us!"

And the worst. We were fighting like two… Like two jealous bitches! That's what we were doing! We were fighting over our men who had, oddly enough, switched places. I was on Cole's side and she was on Neil's! How fucking strange was that? Very.

"Oh, God!" I wailed. "This wasn't supposed to happen."

The waitress, Dena, came over and said, "Girls, I thought it was a bad idea from the get-go."

We turned to her, our mouths open.

"Sure, it sounded good—in theory."

We turned towards each other.

"But then again, anything sounds good in theory."

"Why didn't you say that then?" I asked.

"I don't know," she said. "I kinda just wanted to see how it would turn out."

And how had it turned out? Well, it was a big, old mess, that's how it had turned out. But what to do now?

"Well, let me know when you're ready to order," she said and backed away.

We ignored her departure and stared at each other.

"Oh, shit," I groaned. "Why did we do this?"

"Stupid, stupid, stupid!" she wailed, then stopped and said, "And the ironic thing is, Cole fucked me so good last night I was gasping for air."

I didn't mention that he always fucked me like that. But still. Instead I said, "Neil did the same thing. It was like he's turned into this wild man."

"Cole, too," she said. "He wants it all the time."

I nodded. "Yeah, so does Neil."

She studied me and said, "Do you think that… No."

"What?"

"Well," she said. "Now don't get mad, but do you think that they're still horny for us and it's just kind of seeping over?"

"I don't like the word 'seeping'," I said. "But it might be."

"I don't want to tell you this," she said. "But I think I might have to."

I nodded and waited for her to continue. She didn't, so I snapped, "Tell me!"

"Okay, but promise not to get mad."

"I can't promise that," I said. "Just tell me.

"Okay," she said, drawing a breath. "But just try not to get mad."

"Fine," I muttered.

"I think Neil's going to leave you, Kara," she said softly, then, "I'm so sorry."

Somehow it didn't surprise me. But then again, there was something she needed to know, too. I said, "I think Cole's going to leave you, too. I'm sorry."

She nodded and wiped at her eyes.

I couldn't help but reach across the table and squeeze her hand. "I mean it, Lily, I'm so sorry."

She nodded and wiped at her eyes again. "But maybe it was meant to be like this."

"Maybe."

"He told me he loved me last night," she said.

Cole had told me that awhile ago. I didn't tell her that, though, poor thing. Instead, I said. "But anyway, it doesn't mean..."

"It does, too."

I started to say something but then we just stared at each other for a moment.

"What the fuck is going on with us?" she asked.

"I don't know," I said, looking away. "Are we... Are we..."

She nodded. "I think we are."

"Oh," I breathed and shook my head. "Oh."

"Well," she said. "It was bound to happen. But, hey, our house is almost completely renovated."

"Well, ours was new when we bought it, so it's already done."

"And besides that," she said. "He's got a great retirement account. Y'all will be set up for life."

"We have a good savings," I said.

"Of course," she said. "Your house is a lot smaller than ours is, but, hey, we can add on."

I glared at her. "There is nothing wrong with my house."

"I know," she said. "It's charming."

I nodded.

"I don't think we can be friends after this," she said.

I agreed, "You're right."

"But, hey," she said. "Once the divorces are final, who knows?"

"We know," I said.

"Yeah, you're right. It would just be weird, wouldn't it?"

"It would be *very* weird."

She sighed and stood up. "Just so you'll know, he sent me flowers, too. I didn't tell you cause I didn't want you to get pissed off and tell him to stop sending them."

The little bitch.

"Well, see ya," she said and gave me a brief hug then walked away.

I watched her go. As soon as she was out of sight, I burst into laughter. Not only did I get the better guy, but I got the bigger house! Ha! Served her right, too. After all it was her idea.

I grinned mischievously. Wait until Neil got his seasonal allergies and sneezed his head off all day, on and off. She was going to love that.

Meet, mate and move on.

I went home and sat at the kitchen table and waited for Neil to come home. When he got there, he gave me a sad look and said, "I have to talk to you."

I nodded once and said, "I know you've been having an affair with Lily."

His mouth fell open.

"Save it," I said. "I've been having an affair with her husband, Cole. We met at the Dennis' party about six months ago and we hit it off and had lunch. We started talking about sex and stuff like that and we came up with this plan to screw each other's husbands."

He almost fell over. "You did?"

"Yes," I said. "It just kind of backfired on us."

He was still reeling. "You mean… So, it's like… Really?"

"It is," I said. "We planned the whole thing."

"Wow," he said. "I should have known something was up, though. It was too easy."

"Well, you know what they say about something being too easy," I muttered.

"No, what do they say?"

"Shit! I don't know. I was just saying that. God, Neil!"

He nodded at me and got really quite, then he said, "I'm so sorry, Kara."

"It's okay, Neil," I said gently. "I know we're getting divorced."

He seemed shocked but then he seemed happy, relieved. "Are you okay with that?"

"Oh, yeah," I said. "We'll work out all the details later."

"But," he said. "Are you okay?"

I nodded. "I've never felt better. In fact, I've never been happier since I've been doing this."

"Me either!"

I smiled at him. "It's great, isn't it? Who woulda thunk?"

He cracked a smile and said, "Yeah, who woulda thunk?"

"Well," I said and stood. "It was nice being married to you."

"I had fun," he said. "Who knows? Maybe we can swap out again in a few years."

"I'd like that," I said.

We smiled at each other and shook hands. Life didn't always have to be so complicated. It was nice to know that.

Maybe it was as simple as that we'd learned all we could from one another and there was nothing to do but move on and move forward.

I stared at him. Yeah, I'd miss him. But not his seasonal allergies. Or his cheapness. And that snoring thing he did. Sometimes it sounded like I was sleeping next to a damn Grizzly bear. But I would miss his sweet smiles and his backrubs. But I wouldn't miss his dirty socks at fucking all. Or his inability to pick up after himself. Or…

Ah, it's better left unsaid.

• • •

I climbed into Cole's lap later that night and said, "Meet, mate and move on."

He nodded eagerly.

"You meet someone," I said. "Say, at a bar and you mate—or as you like to say, you fuck."

He smiled and licked at my neck.

"Then you move on," I said and kissed at his lips. "To another conquest."

"But not for a long time," he said, staring into my eyes. "Maybe not ever."

"Right," I said. "Maybe."

He grinned and laid me down and fucked me good. It was always so good with him. And yeah, maybe I'd given up a great man, but I at least I had this one to replace him with. If I so chose. And maybe I wouldn't want to stick with just Cole. Maybe I'd play the field a little. Maybe that's what he wanted to do, too. We could meet up and discuss our findings. Then we could fuck each other. We'd be fuck buddies.

When it was over, we stared up at the ceiling together, holding hands. He turned to me and said, "So, when do you want to get married?"

My eyes nearly popped out of my head. Then I turned to him and said, "Haven't you been paying attention during our lessons, Cole?"

He stared back at me and said, "I think it's mostly bullshit, Kara."

I nodded. He was right. It was mostly bullshit. But that didn't meant I was going to remarry anytime soon. Just in case it *wasn't* bullshit.

"Good night, baby," he said then and gave me a quick peck on the check.

Not two seconds later, he had rolled over and fell asleep. Two seconds after that, he started snoring. It was like I had never stopped being married.

Dirty Story Number Two:

Roughing It

Absolute torture.

It was the anticipation that made me wet. The anticipation of knowing he'd be home soon and after he had eaten his supper, he'd be ready to take me, to take control of me.

I sat at the table and waited. That's all I could do now was wait on him. I glanced at the clock. He'd be home soon, right at five. It was now four-forty-eight. Twelve more minutes. Twelve minutes of absolute torture as I awaited his arrival, as I waited for him to give me that one look, that one look that told me he knew why I was here, he knew why I'd thrown everything away. He knew all about me. And all he knew was that my pussy craved him.

What was it about him? I thought about that and began to heat up even more as I thought about him. It was just him. It wasn't that he was the best looking guy on earth. He was good looking but I'd seen better. That wasn't true. I had never seen anyone who looked like him. He had jet black hair and intense blue eyes. His face was sculpted looking and he had thick red lips that kissed me so brutally sometimes I thought I'd die from the intensity of it. He was tall and he was broad-shouldered. He was built like a Mack truck. He was built to fuck. He was built to fuck me.

I glanced at the clock. It was now four-fifty-one. Nine more minutes. Nine more long, painful minutes. When was he going to get here?

But what was it about him? Him? I thought about it and decided it was the thuggish, "I don't give a shit" attitude that drew me to him. It was the way his eyes looked over me when I stood naked in front of him.

"Umm," I moaned and couldn't help but run my hand across my chest as I thought about him looking at my nude body. As I thought about him coming home and throwing me down on the table and grabbing at me, at my breasts, at my pussy, at me. I put my leg on the chair and opened my legs and touched myself. I was already wet. I was already ready for him. Just the thought of him fucking me did that to me. It didn't matter where I was, either. I could be at the grocery store and think of him fucking me and I'd go wet. Anytime I thought of him, I wanted more of what he'd already given me. Much more.

I stood and began to pace. The clock now read four-fifty-six. Four minutes more and he'd be home. Maybe he'd be early today. Maybe he'd be late. I stopped pacing and thought about that. No, he couldn't be late today. Not today. I'd gone all day wanting him so bad I ached. If he was late, I was going to be pissed.

Just then, I heard his truck pull up. I jumped with excitement, then sat back down at the table, smoothed the calico dress he loved for me to wear—so he could rip it off—and waited. I heard the engine cut off, then the door slam and then I heard him on the front porch. The screen door creaked open and then the front door pushed open. I shuddered with anticipation. He was here. He was home. He would fuck me soon. The torture would be over. I could breathe again. I would be peaceful once I got it. But getting it was the hardest part. That and the waiting.

He walked into the kitchen, threw his black lunchbox on the counter and turned to me. My heart skipped a beat as our eyes locked. *He was home!* He was dirty, as usual, which meant he'd have to take a shower first before anything could happen. Some days, we didn't wait for the shower. I didn't care if he was clean or not. He was a mechanic and he had to get dirty for his job. His nails were sometimes filthy as was his face. I didn't care. I'd rub up against him, getting dirty myself.

"Hi, Ned," I said and smiled at him. "I've got supper ready for you."

His eyes stared at me and looked over my body, over my face. I hoped he liked what he saw. My face was free of any make-up, just the way he liked it. He said he wanted to see me, not a bunch of paint. He liked my full, red lips and my blue eyes and my dark hair. He loved the freckles that were scattered across my chest and my full, pert breasts. He especially liked my ass, which was firm and round. He liked my body, the way I looked. He told me I was beautiful and for once in my life, I believed it about myself.

He nodded once and said, "I see that, Kori."

I waited, and then glanced at the table, at the carefully prepared meal of pot roast, mashed potatoes and gravy, cornbread and sweet tea. A very manly meal made especially for him, my man. I wanted to sweep it off the table with my arm and have him grab me and throw me down. But I didn't. He didn't like to waste food.

"I need to shower," he said.

I almost smiled, then I hid it. I didn't want to seem too eager. He hated it when I was too eager. He liked to pretend it was him that made all the decisions about our fuck sessions. He started them and he ended them. He was in control. Which was fine by me as long as he gave it to me.

"I'll be right back," he said and went into the bathroom to clean up.

I nodded after him and waited. I heard him turn the shower on. As I waited, I pushed the food around on the table, then glanced in the direction of the bathroom. I couldn't stand it anymore. I got up and went into the bathroom and opened the door.

He was standing naked in the old, claw-footed tub. I could see the outline of his magnificent body through the clear vinyl shower curtain. Oh, God. He looked so good. He was so big and so strong. His back was muscled and I loved the run my hands down it as he fucked me. His ass was tight and good. His—

"What is it, Kori?" he asked.

I'd been so immersed in assessing his body, I almost jumped at his words. "Uh, nothing. It's just the food's getting cold," I lied. I didn't give a damn about the food. Besides, we had a microwave.

"I know what this is about."

I stood to attention.

"Go into the bedroom and wait for me."

"No," I said. "It's not that. It's—"

"Go into the bedroom and wait for me," he repeated.

"But—"

"Go into the bedroom and wait for me, damn it."

I went into the bedroom and sat down on the old iron bed. I smoothed the quilt and then fluffed the pillows. I smiled as I looked around the room. It was a whole lot cleaner and nicer than when I'd first seen it. I'd even painted the walls and added a picture here and there to make it nicer. He didn't notice. He was a man and men never noticed stuff like that.

"Turn around and face the bed," he said.

He was behind me, standing in the doorway, a white towel wrapped around his waist. I shivered and turned around.

"Bend over and put your hands on the bed," he said.

I bent over and put my hands on the bed. My ass was turned towards him.

Without another word, he came over and ran his hands over it, pausing to squeeze it as he did so. He kept this up until I was sure I was dripping from being so wet. His hand went under the dress and I shuddered. My skin was bare as I didn't have any panties on. I waited until his hand slid between my legs and rested on my pussy. As soon as it did, I moaned loudly. It was already too much and we were just getting started.

He didn't move for a moment so I began to move against his hand, using it to get off. He pushed the dress up over my hips until my naked ass was in his face and then he nibbled and bit at my ass cheeks as his hand rested between my legs, as I began to grind against it. He stopped suddenly, then pushed my legs further apart and stuck his face between them. I threw my head back in ecstasy. *Mmmmmm…oooh…yes!*

He began to suck me, suck my pussy as I stood over him and ground myself against his face and his mouth. His hands stayed on my ass, gripping it tightly. Suddenly, I couldn't stand it anymore. I came hard and couldn't stop coming. As I came, he pushed me onto the bed and turned me around. My legs went around his waist and his hard cock was in me. I gasped because it felt *so* good.

I grabbed onto his face and began to suck at his mouth as he has sucked at my pussy. His tongue licked at my mouth and then sucked at it as he fucked me.

"Umm," I moaned, unable to get enough. Just then, his head went down to my breasts and he ate at one through my dress. I jerked it open for him and offered him my tit and he took it greedily, grabbing it up in his big hand and squeezing it before his mouth clamped onto it and sucked as hard as he could on my nipple. I threw my head back and a little scream tore from my throat.

He was back at my mouth, his hand still on my breast, squeezing it as he kissed me, as he forced his tongue into my mouth so I could suck on it. It was too much. It felt too good. I was headed into overload. I didn't care. Overload was where I wanted to go. Overload was where that big orgasm awaited.

"Come on," he whispered in my ear. "Come on and do it. Come on and show me what you got in you."

That sent me over the edge, just those few simple words. He wanted me to show him what I could do, what I was capable of. He'd witnessed it before. He liked it. He liked to know how crazy he drove me. How far gone I'd get into it. By me doing this, by me acting like this, he was reassured that he was the only one who could do it, who could send me over the edge. And he was right. He was the only one who'd ever been able to.

I wrapped my legs around his waist and pushed his cock into me as far as it would go. He gasped as I did that. It was almost too much for him. He couldn't handle it. I couldn't handle it. We couldn't handle each other. That's why we wanted it so badly.

Now he was fucking me as I fucked him. He was fucking me hard, just the way I liked it. Our bodies slapped against each other's and our foreheads were pressed together and our eyes open. We stared at each other as we fucked. It was a stare filled with lust and with want and with need. It was a stare that we shared every single time we were together like this, fucking as we were. It was something we shared that communicated what we couldn't in words. It told us that no matter what happened, he was the man and I was the woman. He was my man and I was his woman. Nothing would ever come between us, between this moment. No matter what happened, we'd always have it. We'd always carry it around.

"Ahhh…AHHHH!" I screamed as I came. It was one of those deep-seated pussy orgasms. It was rooted deep within me and he had set it free. I couldn't take it. As much as I wanted it, it almost hurt to let it go.

He was having the same reaction. His body took over and he hissed a little as he erupted inside of me, as his hot cum squirted within the walls of my pussy as he let loose and took me. As he overtook me, as he was overtaken.

Then it was over. He fell on top of me and shuddered. I sighed with satisfaction and kissed the side of his face, then his mouth, then his lips. He opened his mouth and we kissed for a few long moments until we came back down. We kissed and pressed as close as we could get to one another. I'd never felt happier than I did in that moment. I'd never been more content. But then, like most women, I had to go and spoil it.

I stopped kissing him, pulled back and stared into his eyes. "I love you, Ned."

I waited. Maybe this would be the day he'd say it back. I said it almost every day. Almost every day since we'd been together, I'd felt it. Almost every day, I wished he'd say it back.

As usual, he didn't reply. As usual, I got hurt. When would I learn my lesson? Ned didn't say things like "love" or "adore". He didn't have a romantic bone in his body. He was just who he was. I couldn't stand it. I couldn't stand to know I was putting myself out there and he wasn't biting. I couldn't stand to think about loving him when, maybe, he didn't love me back. That tortured me almost as much as waiting for him to come home did.

"Do you love me, Ned?" I asked quietly.

He just stared at me and said, "Let's eat."

And then he was gone into the kitchen as I sat there and let embarrassment sting my face. I'd never learn my lesson.

What the hell had I been thinking?

Well, I hadn't been thinking. I hadn't been using my brain. My pussy had been given the authority to direct my life and I turned all decisions over to it. People always talk about how men let their "little heads" speak for their big heads. Well, I think the same applies to women, too. At least it applied to me.

I don't know what the hell happened to me. All I know was that I met Ned and I didn't look back. All I know was that first moment I saw him, something stirred within me. But most certainly not in the romantic sense. It stirred in my loins, in my pussy. It drove me crazy and made me do things that I would have put other people down for. Things like lying to my husband and meeting Ned at sleazy hotels to fuck the afternoon away. Things like telling everyone I was going to leave my husband to go live with a guy in a rundown house.

Yeah, I'd been married when I met Ned. And, of course, I fucked it all up. Sure, I wanted to have my cake and eat it too. Who doesn't want that? I gave it a shot for a while but it didn't take long before I realized I just wanted to be with Ned. If that meant I would have to rough it for a while and go without the things I'd grown accustomed to, then so be it. I figured things would work themselves out. I didn't care about leaving my life or my husband. I didn't think about the things I would have to give up in order to be with Ned. All I thought about was when he would touch me again.

My family thought I was crazy. Maybe I was. My husband just shook his head, which was weird. But he was the one person who had the least amount of trouble with it. Sure he was upset and told me I was insane and all that, but somehow, he understood. Maybe because he wanted to play around, too. Maybe he was as sick of me as I was of him. I didn't know and I didn't care what he wanted to do. All I cared about was myself. Sometimes people are like that.

My mother wouldn't even talk to me anymore. I'd single-handedly ruined my life, that's what she told me. "You're crazy to leave that good man to move in with that other one! You've worked so hard to get what you have! Why are you doing this? You're going to end up miserable!"

But she was wrong. I'd never been happier.

I left my conscience when I ran off to be with Ned. I left my peace of mind and my luxuries to live in a rundown house with floor that creaked and windows that needed caulking. I left a huge house with marble floors and a gigantic kitchen. I left it all and I didn't look back.

My life before I met Ned had been nice. I was married to a very successful record producer in Nashville. Jim had started out writing songs and moved his way up. Then, one day, he wrote this great tune called *She Walks on Air* and suddenly, we were rich. Well, actually, we wrote it together and I even came up with the title. However, he was the one who did all the legwork to get it produced, so he got all the credit. But I didn't care and I didn't care because we got the big house and the big bank account and the nice vacations that go along with a hit record. We got everything we'd ever dreamed of wanting. All the things that are supposed to make a person happy and content.

Regardless, I was bored out of my skull.

But then something changed. I don't know when, where or how, but it changed and I realized I wasn't as happy as I *should* be. I had always foolishly thought that having nice stuff would make me happy. But now Jim was out of the house more than he was in it. He was a very busy guy. I was left to my own devices. I took up hobbies and I tried my hand at writing songs and learned to play the guitar but nothing left me feeling satisfied, like I was accomplishing anything. I went on shopping sprees and had lunch with the girls. But it was so boring. I was spoiled and when a person's spoiled, nothing really excites them. Nothing really makes them happy. They've got it all but nothing pleases them. So I shopped to fill a void and I tried new things to keep my mind active. I volunteered at the homeless shelter so I would appreciate what I had. I gave money to charities. I did everything in my power to feel happy, to feel like I was supposed to feel and I was supposed to feel blessed. I didn't, though. And I felt a lot of guilt because I didn't appreciate what I had.

Then I met Ned.

I can still remember exactly how he looked the first time I laid eyes on him. He was tall and he was broad-shouldered and he was so good looking. I can remember that my heart skipped a beat and I could hear the blood rushing in my ears. I was suddenly aware of my heartbeat. Aware that I was *alive.*

It wasn't a choice. I had to do it. After I met him, I knew all those fantasies I'd had about other men were just that, fantasies. Like most women, delving off into fantasy land makes marriage more bearable. I would think about having an affair but I never did it. I didn't want to ruin my life. But for him, I ruined it. I was glad to ruin it.

But sometimes I do think if I hadn't met him I could still be living in a nice house and have a big bank account and all the things that make life a little easier. If I had never met him, I would still be with Jim, going to parties and meeting new people. I'd still be eating the best foods and drinking the best liquors and sleeping in the best bed. But I'd still be bored out of my mind. I'd still be looking for something to fill the void and the longing. I'd still be unhappy and I'd still be hating myself.

So, how did I meet him? He fixed my car.

• • •

Jim had bought me a vintage silver Mercedes convertible. It was a nice car but I was afraid to depend on it because it was so old. I would hear this "ding" noise whenever I'd get up to a certain speed. Jim told me it was all in my head but one day, I was driving past this garage near downtown and decided I'd drop in and see if they could fix the "ding".

The sign above the place said "Ned's Garage".

I got out of the car and walked inside, looking around for someone. I heard pneumatic tools being used and could smell the oil being drained from the car right in front of me. I peered around it, looking for someone and said, "Hello?"

"Do you need something?" a voice came out of nowhere.

I jumped, startled, and turned around and there he was. He was wiping his hands off on a blue cloth and was dressed in a mechanics outfit of blue shirt and blue pants and black, thick-soled shoes. As soon as I looked into his eyes, I froze. It was that big of an attraction. I was suddenly aware of myself and began to feel really self conscious. Besides that, I had drawn a complete blank and didn't even know why I was standing there anymore.

He didn't seem to notice that I'd gone blank and said, "Do you need something?"

Just then, two other mechanics came out of the office, gave me the once over and went to the other cars in the garage. I was suddenly aware of everything, of the other guys, of him and of me. I'd never been this self conscious before.

I shook myself a little and tried to smile. As I spoke, my voice shook, "Uh…uh…yeah…uh, my car makes this sound."

He nodded and peered over my shoulder at my car. "Is it the Mercedes?"

"Uh huh."

He walked past me and went to the car. I followed him out, keeping my distance and when he got into the car and started it up, I moved out of his field of vision. I could still see him, but I didn't want him to see me. I wanted to disappear but at the same time, dreaded knowing that soon I'd be on my way back home.

"What does it do?" he asked me.

"When I get it up to around sixty or so, it makes this 'ding' sound." I shuffled my feet and tried to flirt, "Are you Ned?"

"Yeah," he said and started the car. "I'll have to take it around the block. You want to stay here?"

I nodded. Yes, please. There was no way I could have gone with him. I would have fainted if I had gotten that close to him. I shuffled my feet around and was aware of the other mechanics giving me looks. I didn't say anything to them and sat on an old plastic chair outside the office and waited.

He was back in about thirty minutes. I had almost thought he'd stolen the car or something. The more I sat there and waited, the more pissed off I got. I was just about to call Jim and have him come get me when the car roared onto the lot and came to a stop right in front of me.

He got out and said, "I fixed it."

"What was wrong with it?"

"Loose wire," he said.

"Oh," I replied and realized I would have to leave soon. "How much do I owe you?"

"Just go into the office and Louise will write you up a ticket," he said and walked back into the garage without another glance in my direction.

My face stung in embarrassment. Mainly because he didn't give me a second look. Oh, well. I went inside and paid the bill then went home.

I paced a lot during those next few days. All I could think about was him. How could I talk to him? How could I get in the same room with him, alone? But most importantly, how could I fuck him?

Then it occurred to me. I went to the phone and called the garage. That old lady, Louise, answered. I asked for Ned. She said he was busy. I told her he'd worked on my car and I really needed to talk to him about it. She sighed with annoyance and then told me to hold.

I waited forever for him to come to the phone. As I waited, my entire body began to shake with nervousness. I couldn't ever remember being this nervous about anything.

"This is Ned."

I swallowed hard. This was it. I had to do it. I didn't even know what I was doing. What was I doing? I shook myself and tried to speak. I couldn't. Not one word would come out of my mouth. What the hell was wrong with me?!

"This is Ned," he said again with annoyance. "Hello?"

"Oh, sorry," I said so nervously my voice shook. "I had someone on the other line."

"What?"

He wouldn't fall for that. Even so, I proceeded, "It's Kori Clark. You fixed my car a few days ago?"

"Yeah?" he asked, almost disinterestedly.

"Uh, well, it's still making that noise," I said. "Do you think you could have another look at it?"

"Sure," he said. "Just bring it in."

Oh, God. Here it was. Could I do it? Could I go through with it? Could I? I was going to see if I could.

"That's just the thing," I said. "I don't have anyone to drop me off. Could you come by and pick it up for me?"

"Uh," he muttered. "You can't get anyone to drop it by?"

"Well, the thing is," I said. "I can but I need the car day after tomorrow to drive to…uh… Atlanta. Anyway. Everyone I know is out for the day and I wanted to make sure it was running fine before I took that kind of trip in it."

Of course, I wasn't going to Atlanta and I knew plenty of people who'd drop me. He didn't have to know that.

"Oh," he said. "I'll have to charge you extra for that."

"That's okay!" I said eagerly. "I can deal with that."

"Well," he said. "I can send someone by today."

No, no, no, nooooo!

"No offense, but I'd rather you do it," I said. "It's hard to… I just don't… Do you understand what I'm saying?"

"No, I don't," he said. "You want me to come and get the car, right?"

"Right!"

"I guess I can," he said. "But I'm very busy. I don't know what time I can get there."

"I'll be in most of the day," I said. "You can just stop by anytime."

"I guess I could," he said. "I guess I can be by about one or so."

God! He must think I'm some crazy woman! What the hell was I doing? I knew I was being stupid but I just wanted to see him alone. On my own turf. I don't know why, but I did.

"Cool," I replied and grinned. "Let me give you my address."

It seemed to take forever for him to get there. I waited on him all morning. I waited on him until almost two that afternoon. He was late, which meant I was pissed as hell because of it. During that extra long wait, I chastised myself, told myself I was an idiot and I was getting ready to ruin myself over for this mechanic! I also lied to myself. I convinced myself that it would only be once. I would have one afternoon of lust and sex and then he would leave and that would be good enough. But it never works like that. *Never.*

I wanted him to come but at the same time, I didn't know what I'd do once he got there. I was also so excited I kept feeling myself wanting to jump out of my skin. I almost considered calling my doctor and getting a valium. But I didn't.

It was after two when I heard the bell ring. I froze when I heard it. This was it. I couldn't go back no matter what. I'd set this whole stupid thing up. I'd done it all just to get him here and now I couldn't move forward. What the hell was wrong with me?

I forced myself to the front door and when I opened it and saw him, my heart began to beat furiously inside of my chest. So furiously I thought I would pass out.

"Hey," he said. "You got the keys?"

He was very nonchalant. Like he didn't give a shit about anything or anybody. Not even me, which hurt. But that meant he wasn't on to me. He didn't know I'd done all his to get him here. He was just doing his job for some woman who lived in a nice house and drove a nice car. I had a feeling he was going to overcharge me for this.

I nodded and said, "Yeah, come in and let me get them for you."

He sighed and came in.

I turned and looked at him and decided right then and there I was really and truly stupid. God! Look at what I'd done to get this guy here and he didn't even look at me like I was anything. I was more of an annoyance than an object of desire.

"Nice house," he said dryly.

I nodded and grabbed my purse off the hall table and then handed him the keys. "Thanks. Do you think you can have it back by tomorrow?"

He shrugged and took the keys. "I'll see what I can do."

And then he left. As soon as the door was closed, I fell to the floor and wanted to die. I couldn't believe what I'd just done. I was married, for God's sake! Married to a great guy who was…great! And this guy didn't give a shit about anything, that much was obvious. That meant he'd never give a shit about me.

I wanted to slap myself a few times. Instead, I went upstairs and got out of my tight jeans and cute top. I'd even dressed up for him! What an idiot I was! I pulled on a pair of yoga pants and a t-shirt and decided I'd work out a little. But then I heard the doorbell again. *What the hell?*

I raced down the stairs, opened the door and there he was. He looked extremely irritated.

"There is nothing wrong with that car," he said and tossed my keys at me.

I caught the keys and shrugged.

"Listen," he said. "Sometimes you think you hear something but it's in your mind."

What was he getting at?

"That ding or whatever it was is fixed," he said. "Maybe you're not sure of the car and figure 'cause it's so old, it's always about to break down."

He was talking about the car. Oh.

"It should be fine to take to Atlanta," he said. "Now I have to get back to work. Could you drive me over there? Or I can call one of the guys. Whatever you prefer."

I smiled. "I can drive you."

He nodded once.

"Let me change," I said and motioned him in. "It won't take a minute."

He sighed loudly and came into the foyer.

"Why don't you go in there and sit?" I said and pointed at the living room but then wondered if he was dirty from all the grease. I checked him out. He didn't look dirty at all. For a mechanic, he stayed pretty clean.

He went into the living room and sat down. I raced up the stairs, put the outfit I'd had on earlier back on and then raced back downstairs. He was sitting on the couch staring at the wall. When he noticed me standing behind him, he turned towards me and our eyes locked. It was like the first time he'd ever seen me and I knew, just knew, he was feeling a little of what I felt.

Then I heard his stomach growl loudly. Which totally ruined the mood. But still. We'd shared something. I knew we had.

"Sorry," he said and looked embarrassed.

"Are you hungry?" I asked.

He nodded. "Yeah, it's kinda past my lunchtime."

I suddenly felt so bad. I'd made him work though his lunch hour. What a stupid bitch I was! I wanted to make it up to him, to show him I wasn't that bad of a person. I was just losing my mind, that's all. Meeting him had made me lose it.

"Listen," I said. "I know you didn't have to come out here for me or anything and I really appreciate it. Let me fix you a sandwich, okay? Just to say thanks."

"I don't have time."

"For one sandwich?" I asked and started out of the room. "Come on. I make good ones."

He reconsidered and shrugged. "Whatever."

I smiled at him and jerked my head towards the kitchen. He grumbled something under his breath and followed me into the kitchen, sat down at the table and I fixed him a sandwich.

"Do you like everything on it, or just mostly meat?" I asked and took some stuff out of the fridge.

"Everything," he aid. "Listen, you don't have to do this."

"I want to, Ned," I said. "You've really helped me and this is the least I can do."

He shrugged and opened the soda I gave him, took a long gulp and then asked, "Can I smoke?"

"Sure," I said and got him an ashtray. "I quit a few years ago but I don't mind."

"How did you quit?" he asked lit on.

I laughed a little and said, "I went to a hypnotist."

"You did?" he asked and inhaled, then exhaled.

I stared at him. He looked so masculine, so manly, so sexy smoking that cigarette. I wanted him so badly. I shook myself and forced the thought of him throwing me down across the table and fucking me mindless out of my mind.

"Yeah," I said cheerily. "It worked."

"Cool," he said.

"I can give you his number," I said. "If you want to quit."

"And why would I want to quit?" he asked and stared at me.

"I dunno," I said. "For good health."

He chuckled and shook his head. "That's okay."

I shrugged and finished preparing his sandwich. It was huge. I had put a little of everything I had on it. I was almost embarrassed to hand it to him. It was like I making an offering of the sandwich so he'd give me his love.

"Thanks," he said, extinguished his cigarette and took a big bite of the sandwich.

"Let me get you some chips and a pickle," I said and got up and found a pack, then the pickles. I handed them to him and smiled. I realized I liked making a fuss over him. He made me feel girly, like a woman. I hadn't felt that way in a long time.

"Where's your husband?" he asked as he chewed.

"How do you know I'm married?" I asked and sat down opposite him.

He raised an eyebrow and glanced at my wedding ring. I blushed and put my hands in my lap.

"He's away on business," I said. "He goes away a lot now."

"So you're bored?" he asked.

"What do you mean?"

"Without your man around," he said and took another bite. "You're bored."

I didn't take offense as I would have usually done and said, "Yeah, I am."

He nodded once and finished off the sandwich.

"Are you married?" I asked him.

"No," he said. "Not anymore."

I swallowed hard. "What happened?"

"Does it matter?"

I shook my head. It really didn't matter.

He looked around the spotless kitchen and asked, "Do you have a maid?"

"No," I said quickly. "I mean, Jim said we could hire someone but I didn't want to. I like cleaning. I do it all. It really clears my mind up to do menial tasks, you know?"

He stared at me like I was crazy and, maybe, I was.

I went on, not really thinking about what I was saying, "Once you get it clean, it doesn't take that much, you know? Besides, we didn't always have this. We didn't always live here, like this. We struggled for years."

"What happened?"

"He wrote a hit song," I said. "*She Walks on Air*?"

"I know it," he said.

I smiled.

"I hate that song," he said. "It's too sappy."

I blanched. But then I realized why I liked him so much. He was the complete opposite of Jim. The complete opposite of anyone I'd ever met.

He finished off his soda and lit another cigarette, all the while eyeing me. I felt so uncomfortable I almost wanted to run and hide. But I wasn't going anywhere. Even if it was uncomfortable, I was much happier being this close to him than not.

"Yeah, you're a bored housewife," he said. "I've seen it before."

My face flushed and suddenly, I hated him. I hated his masculinity and his piercing eyes that saw right through me.

"Screw you," I hissed.

"Yeah, you want to," he said. "Just like the rest of the women like you."

I should have felt some humiliation. Instead, his comment just piqued my interest. "What does that mean?"

"You think you're the only one who's ever made me a sandwich?"

The humiliation came then. It came so quickly, I wanted to die. I wanted the floor to swallow me up and eat me alive. I wanted out of this room, away from him. But then, why should I leave? If he knew what I wanted, there might be a chance I'd get it.

"Have you done it before?" I asked quietly.

"Done what, Mrs. Clark?" he asked and smoked.

"Call me Kori."

"Done what, Mrs. Clark??"

I stared him dead in the eye and said, "Had sex with another man's wife."

He shook his head. "No, I've been invited but never... No. I never did it."

And there it was. It was out there, in the air. He could grab it if he so chose. He could do whatever the hell he wanted to do. All I would have to do was wait for him to make up his mind.

"Is that what you want?" he asked and put the cigarette out.

I was so ashamed of myself, of wanting it, of wanting it from him. But, even so, I nodded. I think I'd done anything to get it, to just get a taste. If that meant feeling a little humility, then that's what it meant.

"I don't fuck other men's wives."

My head snapped up and I glared at him. How pompous! Well, sure, I wanted it, but how dare he classify me as that, as simply a wife to someone else. How dare he put me in that category?

"Fuck you," I said and felt so much rage I could have slapped him. Then I felt myself do it. I felt my arm going back and then my hand slapping across his face. He didn't flinch. He just sat there after I'd slapped him and stared at me, almost as if it amused him. Then this look of rage crossed his face. Before I could blink, he had my arm and he yanked me out of my chair and threw me across the table. He was bearing down on me, holding me down on the table with his weight.

"Don't you ever do that again," he hissed. "Who do you think you are?"

"Fuck you!" I screamed at him and slapped at him. "How dare you do this to me? I wouldn't ever fuck a man like you."

"And what kind am I?" he asked and grabbed my flaying arms. "Huh? What kind of man am I?"

"A brute!" I screamed. "Let me go!"

He laughed a little and said, "A brute? What does that mean? Does that mean you hate me?"

"Yes!"

"Really?" he asked. "Does that mean you don't want this?"

He placed his hand on my breast. I shuddered. It felt better than I'd anticipated. It felt right. It felt, oh, so right. I wanted more. I sniffed, expecting him to smell like oil and grease but he didn't smell like that. He smelled clean, fresh, like he'd just bathed. It was strange that he smelled so clean. Strange but very nice.

"Does that mean you don't want me to do this?" he asked and put his hand between my legs, right on my pussy. "Huh? You don't want me to do this?"

"No," I murmured.

"Sure?" he asked and grabbed me between my legs and then began to rub at me with his fingers. "If you want me to stop, all you have to do is say the word."

My eyes fluttered open and we stared at each other. He knew I didn't want him to stop. He knew all about me, always would know all about me. And I loved that he knew and I wanted him to know more. I wanted to give him every last molecule of my being and beg him to take it.

"Tell me to stop," he said and rubbed at my pussy. "Tell me to stop this. Go on now and I'll stop."

"Uh…"

"Tell me," he said and bent to nibble at my nipple through my shirt.

"Ummm..."

"Come on, baby, tell me," he said and slipped his hand down my jeans. "Tell me to stop. Tell me to fuck off, that you're going to call the police, that you're going to tell your husband. Tell me to get out of here. Tell me and I'll leave."

"Uh, uh," I moaned just as his fingers slipped inside my pussy.

He leaned down and gave my neck one long lick. "Tell me."

"Don't stop," I breathed and grabbed his face. "Please don't stop."

He didn't, but he did hesitate. There was so much pain for me in that hesitation. What if he changed his mind? I didn't care. I pressed my lips against his and sucked at his mouth until he opened it with a moan. He responded and began to kiss me as his hands grabbed onto my tits and squeezed them just right. I was so turned on I wanted his hands all over my body. I wanted his mouth all over it, too, devouring me like a piece of meat.

"You want me to fuck you?" he whispered in my ear. "Tell me to fuck you."

"Fuck me," I moaned. "Please fuck me."

He pulled back and began to eat at my body. He began to paw at it with his big hands. He tore the clothes from my body until I was naked and squirming beneath him. He leaned back and stared at me, naked and so vulnerable. As he stared, he noticed every single thing about my body the way my chest was rising and falling with the beat of my heart. The way my nipples were erect and pointing at him, wanting his mouth there. The way my pussy swelled and glistened with need and want for his cock. The way my eyes devoured him and wanted him as naked as I was.

I rose up and grabbed him by the shirt and pulled him to me. I pressed my lips against his and we kissed like that, with me naked and him fully clothed. I was offering myself first and that meant he could still turn me down. He wasn't about to.

It didn't take long for me to tear his clothes off his body, for me to sit back and take his body in, the way he had taken mine in. He was such a man. His cock was big and it was hard and it was pointing at me, at my pussy. I wrapped my legs around his waist and pushed it inside me. Once it was all the way in, I threw my head back and moaned with pure delight. It was the perfect fit for me, his cock. It filled me up like no other had ever filled me up.

"Ahh," he moaned as soon as he was in.

"Umm," I moaned and licked at his face, at his mouth. I kissed his neck, then sucked on it, then he pushed my head back and sucked at my neck as we fucked. And fuck we did. We fucked right in the middle of the afternoon on my kitchen table as the plates and soda can rattled as they banged together. We fucked like a man and a woman are supposed to fuck, like animals fuck. It didn't matter. All that mattered was that this is what it all boiled down to, this fucking. It was what we were made for and that made us want it even more. It made us slap up against each other and get every single thing we could out of it.

It didn't take long before I felt the orgasm. It was a hard orgasm, rooted deep in my pussy. It was big one, the biggest I'd ever felt. It didn't tickle or tease. It came at me full force and made me wrap myself around him to get at it. It came at me and hit me like a thunderbolt. It left me speechless, unable to move and to barely breathe. I was sweating and I was drained.

He came then, right after I came. He grabbed me around the waist and pushed everything he had into me. It was a rough fuck; it was vicious but it was sweet. He pumped into me and I could feel his cum rock against the walls of my pussy as he took me and took me over. It meant he was now a part of me and no matter what, he always would be.

When we were done, we didn't say anything. I fell back on the table and he fell on top of me and we laid there for a long moment, breathing hard. I could feel his heartbeat against mine. I sighed because I finally understood something. I understood that no matter what a person attains in life, it would never amount to anything without this. This I couldn't live without. I shouldn't live without. Nothing mattered as much as this and nothing ever would.

He took a deep breath and sighed. I kissed the side of his cheek and said, "Why don't you give me a cigarette?"

Fool in love.

I wanted to be that woman, that woman that drove him crazy. I wanted him to only think of me and when he thought of me, I wanted him to go mad with need. I wanted him to hear a song on the radio and be reminded of me. I wanted him to see other women and think they were me, then be disappointed when they weren't. I wanted to be his everything. I wanted to invade every crevice of his mind.

But I wasn't that woman. He was that man.

He took over my consciousness and all I thought of was him, of wanting him. I wanted him to feel the same way I felt. I wanted him to burn with need for more, the way I burned. And I burned for it.

After our first fuck, I began to see him almost every day, excluding weekends when my husband was home. We would meet at this sleazy motel during his lunch hour. We would never set it up or anything, I just said, "I'll be there at one." And he would come.

I made a fool out of myself, that's what I did. But I didn't care. As long as I was getting what I wanted, I would have done anything. And have been glad to do it.

Sometimes, I'd wait for him on the bed. I'd have my shirt unbuttoned and ready to fall off my shoulders. I would have my skirt hiked up around my hips. I stopped wearing underwear so we wouldn't have to bother taking them off. I would leave all the perfume and make-up at the house after I met him. I'd go aú natural. I'd just wash and comb my hair so it would fall down around my shoulders. I'd be ready when he opened the door.

He would enter the room and, after he closed the door, would stop and stare at me. The way he would look at me made me feel vulnerable, so alive. He would look at me like I was created for him to look at. He would take me in. I'd sit there and let him take me in. I loved the way he looked at me, like he couldn't get enough but he was ready to get started.

I'd slip the shirt off my back. He'd then stare at my breasts, at my nipples. He'd stare a long time, then he'd come over towards me and bend down in front of me. This was the part I loved the best.

His hands came out and began to fondle my breasts. He'd take time to fondle them and then he'd squeeze them. I'd get so turned on I couldn't stand it. But I couldn't move. I wouldn't have moved for anything. He would play with my tits for a long time until my nipples were so hard and erect I thought they'd break off if they got any more stimulation.

Then he'd start nibbling at them. His mouth would move in towards the nipple and I'd grow even more turned on as it came at me. His mouth would clamp onto it and I'd throw my head back and moan a sigh of satisfaction. As he sucked on my nipples, his hands would stay on my breast, squeezing them, holding them, worshipping them. He'd lift them from time to time and lick at the underside. No inch of my skin was left unmarked by his hands or mouth. He covered everything.

As he would do this, his hand would almost sneak between my legs. He'd slide it in and begin to finger me. He'd finger fuck me as he sucked and played with my breasts. It was too much. But he got me off every single time. He knew how to do it so I'd respond. And I'd come every single time. I'd try to hold off so I could enjoy the sensations as much as I could but before I could stop myself, I would come.

When I came, he would push me back on the bed and push my legs apart. Then he'd push his head between my legs and begin to suck at me down there, at my pussy. He would lick and suck and as he did so, he would finger me even more. And, again, it wouldn't take any time before I was coming again and coming hard. I'd grab onto his head and hump his face as he devoured my pussy.

One day, after he was done with me down there, he flipped me over onto my stomach and without a word, he pushed me up on all fours. His hand went between my ass cheeks and I shuddered, knowing what he was about to do. And, yes, I knew what he was going to do. I'd never done this with anyone else. I'd never even thought about doing it. But with him, it came quite naturally.

He ran his hand between the cheeks, grabbing the juices from my pussy until I was good and wet everywhere. I just went along with it, loving the way his fingers teased my ass. I would think he was about to stick a finger in, but then he'd withdraw, driving me crazy. All kinds of murmurs and moans came out of my mouth as he prepared me to fuck my ass. By the time he was finished, I was so ready for it, I was begging.

"Put it in there, baby," I breathed. "Come on."

"Shh," he said and this time pushed his finger into me. I gasped from the pressure but then began to go with it. it felt good. It felt right. I wanted his cock in there, fucking me in the ass. I couldn't stand it I wanted it so bad.

"Do it," I said. "Fuck me there."

He leaned forward and kissed the back of my neck. I gyrated and moaned and hissed with the sensations. I was almost in overload. I didn't know anything, though. I would soon know what real overload was. And it was pure delight.

Then he pulled back and pushed my legs apart. I tensed, not knowing what he was going to do but knowing I couldn't live without it. I felt his cock on my ass and he patted my ass with it a few times before sliding it between the cheeks. That's when I knew there was no going back after this.

It wasn't like I thought it would be. It was much, much nicer. It was like my whole body was on fire and steam was rising from it as pushed his cock deep into me and began to fuck me with it. I felt wild, out of control. I felt like a woman who was being fucked. It felt right being fucked like that. It was a little dirty and a little nasty but a whole lot of fun.

His whole cock filled me up and then I couldn't help but want something else, too, something to grind against. I found my hand on my clit, rubbing it as he fucked me. It didn't take long before I took off and as I came with him fucking me, I began to howl. It was an animal-like cry which came out of my mouth and filled the room. He didn't try to stifle the cry or tell me to hold it down. I think he got some measure of satisfaction knowing he was pushing all the right buttons and knowing he was fucking me in the most intimate way.

Soon he was pumping into me, into my ass as he came. I grabbed onto the bed sheets and pushed my face into the pillow, biting onto it to hold the cries of pleasure inside. As he fucked me, he slapped my ass, hard. I shuddered and wanted another. He slapped it again, this time, he left a print of his palm on it. I loved that and wanted another one and he gave it, just as he came and he came with a grunt and groan. He came hard and after he came, he fell down on my back and we fell to the bed. We didn't move for the longest time. We couldn't move if we'd wanted to. We were too exhausted.

After a few minutes, I turned over and pulled him into my arms and kissed his cheek. I began to kiss him and want him all over again.

"Give me a minute," he said pressed his cheek next to mine.

"Okay," I said and loved the feeling of being so close to him. I loved his smell and his deep blue eyes and I loved…him. Before I could think or stop myself, I said, "I love you."

He didn't move for the longest time, then, when he did, he moved away from me. I was almost in shock. What the hell had I been thinking? Why did I have to go and ruin it all? But then I got pissed off. What was wrong with him? And why hadn't he said it back? He told me he didn't do stuff like this, that he'd never considered having sex with another man's wife until he met me. Didn't that make me special? Didn't that mean something? Apparently not.

Just to be sure he understood what I'd said, I hissed, "I said I love you, Ned."

"I heard you the first time."

"You bastard!" I yelled and pushed him away from me. "What the fuck is wrong with you?"

I started to slap him but he grabbed me by the wrists and pulled me down until I was beneath him, struggling to get him off of me.

"I said I heard you," he said. "Don't make an issue of it."

"Don't make an issue?" I spat. "I just—"

He put his hand over my mouth and said, "Let's not go there, Kori. Let's not do that."

I glared at him and decided I would never see him again. I was never going to let him touch me or look at me or anything else. I swore to myself that I'd never tell him that again. *Never!*

"Now I have to get back to work," he said and stood from the bed.

I wanted to kill him.

He dressed quickly and then let himself out of the room. I broke down and cried as soon as he was gone. I hated him so much. I'd put myself out there and I'd gotten burned by this asshole. Never again, I promised myself as I dressed and headed home. Never again would I call him or think about him or anything.

It worked for a while. I mean, a few hours. The next day, I was in the motel room again waiting on him and when I heard him at the door, I couldn't help but smile and convince myself that I'd eventually win him over.

I was such a fool. But that's what love does to the best of us. It makes fools out of us.

After we were done that day, he said to me, "I can't do this anymore. If you want to see me, you're going to have to choose between me or your husband. I don't like doing this because it was done to me, by my ex-wife. Sorry but you have to make your choice. This is the last time I'll meet you here."

"Are you serious?" I asked.

He nodded. "You know I am."

I briefly wondered what he meant, then I got it. "Do you want me to…?"

"You can move in with me, if you like," he said. "If not, whatever."

"Do you love me?" I asked because, I thought, surely, if he wanted me to move in with him, he loved me.

"I told you I wasn't going to talk about that," he said. "Now I have to go."

I watched him leave and felt lost. But I knew what I was going to do. It wouldn't have taken a genius to figure out what I did. I felt bad about doing it, about leaving Jim, but then again, when you're addicted to someone in the way I was addicted to him, nothing but being with that person makes sense. And it makes sense because when you're with them, you feel whole again.

My new life.

I stared around the small house. It was pretty rundown, but it looked better than when I'd first moved in. I'd done what I could, but it was still so cramped, especially since I'd moved in some of my stuff. I stared at my guitar in the corner. I hadn't picked it up since I'd moved in. I hadn't had the desire, really. Song writing was mostly born out of unfulfilled desires, especially country songs. When a person is in the mist of a full-blown love affair, it takes front stage and everything else takes a backseat.

The house was on the outskirts of Nashville. It sat in the middle of twenty or so acres Ned had bought right after his divorce. He said he kept meaning to fix up the house but never got around to it. It was only him, after all. And he worked a lot.

Our life was pretty routine. He'd get up early to go to work. I'd hear him in the shower and the thought of him touching me would take over. I'd get up and join him. We'd kiss for minutes as the hot water beat down on us. We'd kiss and touch each other all over as the minutes ticked away. Soon, his hands would go between my legs and then all bets were off. He'd get out of the tub and then he'd back me down the hall, all the while kissing me, and into the bedroom where he'd throw me down on the bed and fuck my brains out.

If for some reason I slept through his shower, I'd get up and clean the house and then sit around and wait for him to come home. Some days I went shopping, but I didn't have any money anymore and couldn't buy anything. My divorce wasn't final and Jim had frozen all of our assets to keep me from "running though with our life savings". He wanted to make sure he got his part. I couldn't even take anything out of the house.

In the meanwhile, I was totally dependent on Ned. He would give me money and all that, but I didn't feel right spending it. I was getting the best part of him anyway, and anything in addition to that would make me feel ingratiated. I hated that feeling and almost got a job but he told me not to worry about it. And I didn't because once my divorce went through, I was going to very well off. Then I could build us a nice house on his land. That was, if he'd let me.

Ned's house wasn't so bad. It was just so old and cold. I shivered and froze during that winter I moved in with him. I got a little portable heater and moved it around room to room with me.

I never went to see him at work. I felt weird about that as that's where we met. Also, I didn't like the lady who ran the office. She was a mean old bitch and whenever I called for Ned, she'd snap, "Is this that girl who left her husband for him?"

Nothing much happened as I waited for him to come home at night. Mostly, it was just me and the TV. One day, I was sitting watching TV when I heard someone pull up outside. I peered out the window to see my best friend, Elise, pull up in her BMW. I was almost in shock. I hadn't spoken to her after I'd told her I was leaving Jim. She told me I was crazy and that I had better reconsider.

"Men like Jim don't come around very often," she told me.

"Neither do men like Ned," I said.

"Girl, I am telling you, you are making a mistake."

"Well, it's my mistake to make."

She rolled her eyes and said, "Listen, Kori, I know what you're doing and you're not fooling anyone."

"And what am I doing?"

"You're in love with his dick," she said. "You're not in love with him."

"Yes, I am," I said. "I've never felt anything like this before."

"Oh, come on," she said. "Get over yourself. All women go through this. Fuck him on the side but leave your life alone."

"What do you mean?" I had snapped at her, getting so pissed off I couldn't see straight. She didn't know what I was going through. This was real. This was love, even if Ned wouldn't say it to me, I believed he felt it. And that's all that really mattered. The way he communicated was through fucking and through our fucking I knew he loved me. He had to. There was no way he could make me feel the way he did if he didn't. Could he?

"I think it's called hitting your sexual peak," she said. "All women go through it and once you hit it, you want more sex."

"Have you gone through it?" I asked.

She smiled shyly and said, "This isn't about me, honey, it's about you. Meet him and have your fun. Believe me, in six months, you'll be bored with him and wonder why you wanted to leave Jim in the first place."

But she had been wrong. The six months were up and I was still so in love with Ned couldn't think straight. And to think he didn't love me back was unbearable.

He was perfect. No, he wasn't. I wanted him to be perfect, so I made him perfect in my mind. He would have been perfect if he loved me. But he didn't. He never said it, even when I said it to him. Even when I begged him to say it, to validate my feelings, he wouldn't. Not only that, he refused to. The first time I'd told him I loved him had been the worse. I got so sick afterwards, I raced into the bathroom and threw up, then I started crying again. Isn't that what love does to you? It did it to me. It made me sick—physically sick.

It didn't seem so long ago, but it was almost six months. Six months of sheer hell as I wondered why I loved him and he didn't love me back.

"I love you," I said. "And you don't love me. This relationship isn't going anywhere."

"If you walk out that door," he said. "Don't ever come back."

I dropped my head to my chest and nodded. The tears in my eyes spilled out and fell on my face as I looked back up at him and said, "What's so wrong with me?"

"I've told you," he said. "I don't say stuff like that."

"Because you don't feel it," I said.

"No," he said. "Because it's not necessary. You should know how I feel by now and if you don't, then that's not my problem."

"You bastard!" I screamed at him. "How could you do this to me?"

He just sat there and stared at me, as if he were trying to figure me out. I understood that he thought these were just words, that they didn't mean anything. But they meant something to me. And for him not to respond killed me like nothing else. It wasn't just a stab in the heart; it was a stab all over the body, mind and soul. It hurt like absolute hell.

I realized he didn't love and he didn't love me because it was my Karma. I'd hurt and disappointed people to be with him. I'd hurt myself. I'd given everything away to run off with him. By him not loving me, I was just getting my payback.

And when I convinced myself he didn't love me, it made me love him even more. I loved him so much I hurt over it.

I shook myself just as Elise got out of her car and headed towards the front door. I looked around the living room, at all the old furniture and hoped she wouldn't make fun of it.

I took a breath, opened the door and said, "Just what the hell brings you out here, girl?"

She grinned and shook her head. "I just wanted to see you since you don't call anymore."

I felt bad for an instant but then realized she didn't call me either. I had given her my new number and still had my cell phone. But then I knew it was me. I didn't want anything from my old life to interfere with my affair.

"Come here and give me a hug," I said and opened my arms.

She grinned and we hugged, then went inside. As soon as I closed the door, she said, "Good God! What a fucking dump!"

I blushed and then said hurriedly, "As soon as I get my money from the divorce, I'm going to build a better house."

"Yeah and tear this one down," she said and took off her coat and scarf. She was a small woman, like me, but had auburn hair and ivory skin. She couldn't even think about going out in the sun without burning. Her husband was a studio musician. He traveled all the time, too.

"Sit, sit," I said and motioned her to the couch. "Tell me what's been going on."

"Not much," she said and sat down. "I'm bored, as usual. Of course, Wayne is gone again and well… It's winter. What can you do in the winter?"

"Not much," I said.

"Not much?" she replied and raised an eyebrow. "Listen, honey, I know what *you've* been doing."

I blushed again.

"Anyway," she said. "I wanted to tell you I went by Ned's garage and got a look at him."

"Elise!"

She nodded. "I think I understand now. I bet he's got a big one, doesn't he?"

"Oh, God!" I groaned. "Don't ask me that."

"Well, don't tell me then," she said and lit a cigarette. "Oh, sorry. I forgot you don't smoke anymore."

I sighed and pointed at an ashtray.

"You started smoking again? After all you went through to quit?"

I nodded. "I'm an addict."

"Well, here then," she said and handed me her pack.

I smiled and lit one. We smoked for a few moments, not saying anything. We'd had a really big fight when I left Jim. She thought I was stupid for doing it and maybe I was.

"You know this place isn't too bad," she said. "I mean, it's got a certain country charm to it. Some of this furniture must be antique."

I shrugged. "I don't know. Tell me what's been going on."

"Nothing much," she said. "All the other girls want to know what's going on with you. We still meet for lunch about once a week. Your ears must burn a lot."

I nodded. I had a feeling they were all talking about me. I remembered our lunches. We'd talk and laugh and smoke and drink and gossip and have the best time. All the chicks I hung out with had husbands in the recording industry so we all had a lot of time to ourselves. We'd go out at night sometimes and flirt and dance with other guys. We'd go to the Waffle House for breakfast afterwards and just have the best damn time.

"You should come to lunch next week," she said.

I nodded. "Maybe I will."

She smiled at me and said, "Well, you've never looked better, Kori. Roughing it certainly agrees with you."

I didn't take that as a compliment because I knew she didn't mean it as a compliment. And I could tell she was a little jealous. She'd seen Ned, hadn't she? She was a woman and she understood that sometimes being with a man like that was much better than having nice things.

"So are you going to stay with this guy?" she asked and put her cigarette out.

"I don't know," I said. "I think so."

"You think so?"

I shrugged. "Are you hungry? I could make us a sandwich."

"No," she said. "I'm fine. I'm still on that diet I told you about."

"Is it working?"

"Yeah, until I go into the kitchen at night and eat all the cookies."

We laughed.

"I just wanted to see how you were," she said and stood. "I really have to go."

"Well, you can stay for a while, can't you?" I asked.

"No," she said. "I have to get back. It took me forever to drive out here. I got lost several times."

"How did you know where this place was?"

"I told you," she said. "I stopped by and asked Ned."

"No," I said. "You just said you saw him."

"Well, I also talked to him," she said and put on her coat. "He doesn't talk much, does he?"

I shook my head. He didn't talk too much but sometimes we'd have a good conversation. Most times, when we were together, we were fucking and when you're fucking you don't usually try to carry on a conversation. Unless, of course, you're talking dirty.

"Well," she said at the door. "I hope you're happy."

"I am," I said and hugged her. "Come back soon."

"Maybe I will," she said. "When's your divorce final?"

"Actually, in a few days," I said. "Jim finally agreed to let me have half of our savings."

"Good for you," she said. "If I ever divorced Wayne, I'm going to bleed that fucker dry."

I laughed and shook my head at her. "You should. But, besides, I helped him write that damn song, after all."

"You did?"

I nodded. "I did. In fact, I gave him the title. I couldn't prove it in court or anything but he knows it."

"Wow," she said. "I had no idea. It's such a good song, too. Maybe you should write another one or something."

"Maybe I should," I said and smiled at her. "Give me a call sometime."

"Will do," she said and left.

I watched her get into her car and waved. She waved back and pulled away. I knew I'd probably never hear from her again.

I realized I'd given up so much to be with Ned. And I still didn't know if he loved me or not. Surely he did. He just couldn't verbalize it. Or wouldn't.

I couldn't fight it.

Of course, Elise was right. I had hit something once I turned thirty. I don't know what it was, but I suddenly felt so sexual. Whether that meant I hit my sexual peak or whatever, I didn't know and I didn't care. All I knew was that it drove me absolutely mad, this urge, this desire. I tried to fight it but that was no use. I didn't tell anyone about it. I just kept it hidden and started to fantasize about almost every guy I laid eyes on.

Oh, yeah, I did that. I'd scope out guys, look at them, want them. It felt right to look at them like that, to want them. I never made a move, of course, but I felt it. It felt right to feel it, too.

They wouldn't even have to glance at me and I'd get excited just thinking about them throwing me down and fucking my brains out. I was in such a fever pitch all the time it's a wonder I didn't fuck around more—or sooner. By the time I met Ned, it's like I *had* to do something. It's like if I didn't, I'd die. If it meant screwing up my life and fucking with my security, then that's what it mean. If it meant hurting other people, I didn't care. So when I met him, it was like everything finally fell into place. I'd been looking for someone for a very long time and it just seemed like the heavens dropped him out of the sky and into my life.

However, getting a gift that big does come with a price. The price had been the ruination of my marriage. I thought about how I had hurt Jim. We'd been together so long. I hated that I hurt him. I hated myself for that, but if I could have taken the need and done away with it, I would have in a heartbeat. I didn't want to give up my comfy life anymore than he wanted me to leave. It's not that I hated my life or anything. Who in their right mind would give up the kind of life I'd given up? No one. But I did because I couldn't fight my urges anymore.

But Jim and I had fought for years and looking back, I realized this was the reason we were fighting all the time. It wasn't about the bills or the toilet seat. It was about me feeling like I'd been put in a cage. I'd think of reasons to get pissed off at him so I could yell some of the frustration out—to force him to set me free.

We were both victims of our vows, our commitment. I think he wanted to screw around as much as I did and looking back on it, I sometimes think he did screw around on me. He just didn't say anything. Men can do that, can't they? Put a bone in front of a dog and he'll always take a bite.

I found it very unfair, all of it. It's like women are supposed to be chaste while men can just be themselves. No one really expects better of them, do they? It's not fair, but that's the way it seemed to be. It's no wonder I was so confused when I hit my thirties. It's no wonder I drove myself and my husband crazy. I didn't know what to do! So many things were dictated and the options were limited. Damned if you do and damned if you don't. But everyone always sees sexuality as a bad thing and not as the byproduct of nature that it is. If everyone would get over their sexual hang-ups, we'd all be much happier. I know I would have done it sooner and given myself peace of mind if I hadn't thought I was hurting others. But I was taught to always think of others before myself. And I readily did. It got me nowhere.

I wasted so much time denying what was in my heart, what was in my gut. It was an instinct to chase something though I dared not name it. I didn't dare tell myself I wanted other men. And I didn't dare because I was scared shitless that I'd fuck up my life.

But I did try to deny it. I tried to bury it. I tried to sleep it off. It did no good. The life was being slowly sucked out of my marriage and it was being sucked because, maybe, that's the way it's supposed to be. We grew apart, perhaps, because we were meant to grow apart. That didn't keep us from grasping at our dying relationship and trying to revive it. We were both afraid to make the first move, even though it was the cause of a lot of our fights.

I still felt like shit about it. Jim had been so good to me, so hurt when I'd told him I was leaving.

"Don't go," he had said. "We can work it out."

But that was the problem. I didn't want to work it out. There was nothing to work with. I couldn't wait to get away. I couldn't wait to get into Ned's bed permanently.

We fought about it; we yelled and screamed at the top of our lungs. I cried and begged Jim to be more understanding. I begged him not to take it personally.

"How can I not?" he had hissed. "You're dumping me for a fucking mechanic!"

I hated that he had to make a dig at Ned like that. I hated myself for feeling I had to defend Ned. I hated myself. But I couldn't deny it and neither could he. In the end, I think Jim understood what was going on. He didn't like it one bit, but he understood. I hated what I was doing to him, but I couldn't *not* do it. I had to do it; otherwise, I would have gone insane.

Love had very little to do with it. I loved him, sure I did. Still do. The fire of the relationship had simply gone out. That's all. I think we were both shell shocked from it. How could this have happened to us? What happened to our happy union? All we could do was watch our love slip away.

I knew if it hadn't been Ned, it would have been someone else. But I still missed my life from time to time. And I missed Jim. Not all the time, but occasionally. I missed the security. We had been so close once. I hated that we had to turn into bitter enemies just because our marriage was over. I think that's what's expected of all of us. Get married, get divorced, then hate each other for the rest of our lives.

All of this is marriage's dirty little secret. No one ever says they divorce because of hormones or biological imperative. No one ever admits to wanting others. They don't have to. They can keep it to themselves but most of us know better. We know why we do the things we do and it certainly isn't because we've suddenly become "incompatible" with our significant other. If we were that incompatible, we wouldn't have hooked up in the first place.

But it was my hormones taking over. Nothing I could do about it, either. So I didn't. If that made me a homewrecker, then that's what it made me. But it was my turn to do what I wanted to do. It was my life, I kept telling myself; it was my life to do with what I wanted. And what I wanted was Ned, day and night; I wanted him all of the time. I wanted to do it just for the pleasure of doing it.

I realized it wasn't doing me or Jim any good to be this miserable, so I left. Maybe then, we could both move on with our lives.

And Elise had felt what I was feeling, too. She was just too chicken shit to admit it. She didn't understand that getting older meant the years were slipping by and it was time to do something about it. I made up my own mind to do something about it. There was a reason I was put on earth and this was it. When I finally got the balls to do something, it was very liberating. I knew it would be, too.

It might have driven me crazy, but I couldn't verbalize it to anyone. I fought with it until… Until I met Ned.

• • •

All of that seemed less important once I met Ned. Suddenly I could see myself doing him, fucking him. He was the first guy I'd run across that I was willing to make a fool of myself over. He was the only guy I'd throw everything away for. What was it about him? What made him so special?

He just... He was just... Ummm... He was ummmm. That's what he was—ummmm. He was the kind of guy all women wanted. He was every woman's fantasy. He was pure sex. That was the reason I had to have him. I wanted to stake my claim on him.

And to think, he didn't even love me.

I shook the thought out of my head. Of course, he loved me. How could he not? He just couldn't... He couldn't say it.

Maybe I could write a song about him. I thought about that. What would I write? About the way he made me feel? About the way he looked at me? About how I would go crazy just knowing he was coming home to fuck me? Now that would make a great song. He could be a foot away from me and I would get shivers down my spine. He wouldn't even have to do anything and I'd be ready for him. He made all those other guys look like dopes. He made everyone in the world seem less important.

I picked up the pen and stared at the blank piece of paper. It had been a long time since I had tried to write a song. Could I do this?

He gives me so much
So much love, light and air
If he only knew
If he only knew what his touch meant
To me
If he knew, he might run and hide

I stopped writing and shook my head. It was hard to get back into it. I shouldn't have ever stopped writing. But then, it became less important when I met Ned.

Everything became less important.

I got up and rummaged around until I found the CD with *She Walks On Air* on it. I popped it in and smiled to myself. It was my song. The one my husband had written for me. Actually, the one I'd helped him write. It came on and the singer, a cute country boy named Ted, crooned. He had the sweetest voice. I sang along with him and smiled to myself after it finished.

"Now that's a song," I said and glanced outside at my car. For some reason, I felt like celebrating. I felt like picking Ned up for lunch and then maybe going to a sleazy motel. I needed something to inspire me. He could do that.

I dressed hurriedly and raced out the door. Soon, I was on the interstate and headed towards his garage. For some reason, I turned off before I got to the exit and decided to take a little drive in the suburbs. I drove and drove, listening to the radio, just enjoying being out of the house. Then I glanced at the sign on the street. I was on Maple! I was only a few miles from my old house. Without thinking, I turned the car left and drove to the house. As I pulled up in front of it, I got a little sick, thinking about how much I'd given up to be with Ned.

What was I doing here?

I stared at the house and felt a surge of pride. We'd earned that house together, every last brick, every last leaf on every shrub. We'd worked so hard. Now it was gone. I'd let it slip right through my fingers.

I shook myself. What the hell was I doing here? I hurriedly put the car in reverse. Just then, Jim came out of the front door and stopped, staring at me. Then he smiled this happy smile, like he was really glad to see me. Oh, no. I wasn't here to reconcile. I was here to… I don't know what the fuck I was doing here. I just knew I wasn't supposed to be.

"What are you doing here?" he called and came over to the car.

"Nothing," I said. "It was weird. I listened to our song and… Nothing."

"Wanna come in for a drink?"

"I thought we were fighting," I said.

"Well, we can take a time-out," he said and opened the door. "I won't tell if you won't."

"Okay," I said. "Just one drink."

"How have you been, Kori?"

I smiled at him. Couldn't help it, really. He was so cute and so nice and… So going to be my ex-husband soon.

"I've been okay," I said. "You?"

"Great," he said and really smiled at me. "It's good to see you."

And to think the last time we'd seen each other, we'd been so angry we'd been foaming at the mouth.

"You, too," he replied and opened the front door.

I walked in and tried not to get sick at the sight of the beautiful house. It was so clean and new and so not mine anymore. I turned to Jim and smiled. He smiled back. Maybe he was going to let the divorce go through now. Maybe he wasn't mad anymore.

"Come on into the kitchen," he said. "I've got some beer."

I followed him into the kitchen and sat down at the table. I glanced at it and remembered Ned fucking me on it. I pulled away and took the beer from Jim.

"So what's shaking?" I asked and took a sip.

"Nothing much," he said and sat down. "What's going on with you?"

"Same," I said. "I'm trying to get back into writing but it's not working."

"Just keep at it and it'll come," he said. "You were always too good to let it go to waste."

What a sweet thing to say! I wanted to lean over and kiss his cheek but I didn't. Instead, I gave him another smile, which he retuned. We hadn't smiled at each other like this in years.

"So anyway," he said. "How's…"

"Ned," I said. "He's fine."

He nodded. "Good to know."

"Jim," I said. "Listen, I don't know why I drove all the way over here. I guess I just want us to be cool again, you know? I hate this bitterness and the fighting."

"I hate it, too," he said. "Not that it's so unlike us or anything."

We laughed quietly. We had gotten into some major fights over the years.

"But anyway," he said. "I'm tired of fighting over money. I think it's time we settled, don't you?"

My mouth fell open. Hallelujah! Praise the Lord! I knew it was a good time to come here! I knew something good was going to happen today!

"I can't tell you," I said. "How happy that makes me."

"It makes me happy, too, Kori," he said.

"That's just great," I said, smiling. I couldn't stop smiling. "So what made you change your mind?"

"I've met someone," he said and smiled. "You were right. I'd forgotten how wonderful it is to…you know…"

My smile faded.

"So I'm not going to fight with you anymore," he said. "We're going to settle, get it done with, and get on with our lives."

"Oh," I said and stared at my beer, then picked it up and downed it. "Great."

"I'm not mad anymore," he said. "In fact, I don't know why I was so pissed off to begin with."

I nodded and felt a little sick. I'd brought this on myself. Definitely no going back now.

"What I'm trying to say," he said and touched the top of my hand. "Is that I'm sorry I was such a bastard."

I nodded.

"It's weird," he kept on. "But I feel so good about everything now. Now I understand what you were saying. I got it then, too, but now I really get it."

He was going to have to shut up. So what if that made me a hypocrite? Big deal. He was my husband once and I didn't want to hear about him falling in love with someone else, especially since the guy I was in love with me probably didn't love me back. Life could be such a bitch!

"Who is she?" I asked quietly.

"Oh, no one you know," he said. "She's a backup singer right now, but is going to be cutting a record real soon."

"Of course, you'll be producing, right?" I said, getting so jealous I couldn't see straight.

"Huh?"

"You'll be producing, right?" I said. "How long have you known this great singer?"

"What are you getting at?" he asked, then nodded like something just occurred to him. "Oh, I get it. You go out and cheat on me, so you obviously think I did the same thing. I can tell you right now, I never did and I don't really care if you believe it or not."

I swallowed hard. "But obviously, this girl is somebody, right? She's on her way up."

"She might be."

"What the hell does that mean?" I snapped.

"What?" he asked. "Oh, I get that, too."

"What?"

"You're jealous," he said. "And I thought you'd be so happy to see me move on."

But I wasn't happy! I was miserable! Why couldn't I just be happy, for him, for me? This was what I wanted! I didn't know. I didn't know what was wrong with me.

"Oh, I am happy," I said and forced myself to smile at him.

"I'm glad," he replied, eying me suspiciously.

I stared at him and wondered why I wasn't doing a celebration dance instead of being a pissed off bitch. But what had I expected? Oh, that was easy. I had expected him to wait around on me, even when I had no intention of going back to him. Of course, I had wanted him to pine over me. It was wrong and immature, but I had wanted that. I was a bitch. I was *such* a bitch!

"Oh, would you look at the time," I said and stood. "I really have to go, Jim."

"Okay," he said and stood. "Let me walk you to your car."

I gave him a tight smile and we walked to my car in silence. Once I got in, he held the door open, then leaned down and kissed my cheek. That gesture told me it was really over.

"Take care, Kori," he said quietly. "And if you ever need anything, I'll be here for you."

"I know," I said. "Thanks, Jim."

"I'll call my lawyer later on today," he said. "We should be able to tie all this up within a week."

Now he was in a hurry. Now he wanted to tie everything up, nice and neat. Now he didn't want to fight anymore. Now I was all alone. For good.

"Great," I said. "Sounds good."

"And who knows?" he said. "After it's all said and done, maybe you and Ned can cover over and have dinner with us."

With us? Was he planning on moving that bitch into my house? The bastard. I knew if I didn't get out of there quick, I might run him over with the car. Sometimes he just didn't know when to shut his big mouth.

"Sounds good," I said and closed the door, then waved at him. He waved back and I got the hell out of there as fast as I could.

As I drove, I started to cry and then I started to sob. I was out of control. I had no idea that when the final strings of my marriage were cut that I'd be at a loss. I had no idea I'd hurt so much over it. I knew it was selfish way to be but I couldn't help it.

I had to see Ned. I needed his arms around me. I needed to hear his voice to take this pain out of my heart. I sped up and it seemed to take forever to get to his garage. I got stuck at every red light.

Finally, as I neared the garage, I began to calm down. It was no big deal. Everything was going to work out for the best.

As soon as I pulled into the parking lot, I noticed that Ned was talking to someone just outside of the office door. That someone was a very attractive blonde woman. She was built like a brick shithouse. He nodded at her and seemed to be listening intently to everything she said. Then he leaned down and kissed her cheek! The bastard! After a minute, she got into her car and left.

I was left stunned. What the hell had just happened? Was he sleeping with that woman? He could be! He could be fucking around on me all the time and I'd be oblivious. I realized that this whole affair had done nothing but make a fool out of me.

I had lost twice today. First my ex and now my current. This absolutely sucked—bad. And I'd brought it all on myself.

Before he could see me, I put the car in reverse and backed out. Then I drove like a bat out of hell out of there. I had to get home. But where was home? Where was home now?

Jealous bitch.

I went back to Ned's place and started to pack. By the time he got home, my car was loaded. I didn't know where I was going and I didn't know what I was going to do, but I couldn't take this shit anymore. If Jim got to fall in love with someone else and have them love him back, I got to, too. That person, I realized wasn't Ned. For whatever reason, he didn't love me. Nothing I could do about it, either.

"What's that all about?"

I stood up from the bathroom vanity and said, "What?"

"Your car is packed," he said. "What's that all about?"

"It's about me leaving you," I said and turned to him.

His eyes narrowed. "What the fuck are you talking about?"

I stood and grabbed my make-up bag, then turned on him. "I know you don't love me, Ned. I also know I've made a complete disaster of my life. I threw everything I had away with both hands to be with you. Everything I had worked my ass off for. And for what? So you can make a fool out of me? I don't think so."

I started past him, but he grabbed my arm and halted me. "Tell me what's going on, Kori."

I looked him right in the eye and said, "I saw her."

"You saw who?"

"Her," I said and pushed him away from me. "Now if you'll let me go, I'll be out of your hair."

He let me go. But then he came after me and stopped me at the front door. I ignored him and opened it. He shut it. I tried again, this time, he blocked it.

"Move!" I yelled and tired to wiggle past him. I knew I should have just left a note on the kitchen table. But he didn't even deserve that! I knew, also, that I had stayed just so I could tell him off. And I was definitely going to do that.

"No," he said. "Tell me why you're leaving."

"I told you," I said, getting pissed off. "I saw her."

"Who?"

"That woman," I hissed. "Today, at the garage. You kissed her cheek."

He just stared at me, not taking the bait. Sometimes, I hated him so much. I couldn't take it anymore. I wanted to yell and I wanted to scream and I wanted to hurt him.

"So, who was she?!" I screamed, hating the sound of my own voice.

"My ex," he said calmly. "She came by to ask for some money. I gave her a couple a hundred."

Oh, God, I was turning into one of those bitter, resentful, jealous women. I was a jealous bitch! I was a freak! I was so jealous of him I couldn't see straight.

What drove me crazy was the way he kept me hanging on. He didn't deny or confirm any feelings. He just let me make a damn fool out of myself. He didn't validate me or my feelings. I was so unsure of myself and of our love. I was going insane.

"I haven't fucked her in years," he said. "If that's what you're wondering."

Before I could stop myself, I drew back and slapped him hard across the face. He didn't even flinch. It was almost as if he expected it.

"I'll take that one," he said. "But only that one."

I tried again. I wanted to slap him and hurt him and pull him down to my level so bad. I wanted him to feel the pain I felt, the pain of loving someone who didn't love you. I wanted him to crawl and beg and plead.

He grabbed my arms, twisted me around and held me tight. I fought with him for a few seconds, then I gave up. I wasn't going anywhere. He was too strong.

"Now let's get this over," he said.

"It is over."

He sighed. "Kori, I have had a very long day. Let's not do this."

I moved out of his arms and turned on him. "It's all about you, isn't it? Your long day, your ex-wife, all of it. It was never about me or about what I wanted."

"Come on," he said. "That's bullshit and you know it. You get what you want."

I started to cry. "No, I never do, Ned. I never get what I want. What I wanted was a man who loved me, that's all. And I had one. I had one that worshiped me and now he's gone because of you! I wish I'd never met you! You ruined my life!"

He dropped his head. I was getting what I wanted. I was getting to hurt him the way he was hurting me. I was getting to reject him. I hated it, too. I hated everything and everyone. But mostly I hated myself. Maybe I didn't deserve happiness.

"It isn't enough, Ned," I said. "I can't do this anymore."

He nodded. I walked to the door, picked up my make-up bag and stopped. I wanted him to tell me to stay but when he didn't, I wasn't surprised at all.

A week after I left Ned, my divorce went though. I was a free woman. I was finally unmarried again.

Not that it did me a damn bit of good.

For the first time in my life, I was on my own. I was alone, independent. If I watched my money, I could live a nice life and never have to work again. But I didn't care. I needed to work. I needed something to occupy my mind.

I got a nice loft apartment and began to furnish it. I took my time and bought things I liked. It was good to do that, to not have to compromise or fight over the style of a couch or bed.

The nights were very long for me. It was worse because the feelings I had for Ned were still there, lying dormant, torturing me. It was worse than when I'd divorced Jim. Way worse. It was like I was killing part of myself. It was like I had amputated my own arm and all I could do was stare at it as it gushed blood. It was like I was ripping my own heart out and setting it on fire. All I could do was watch it burn.

A month went by. A long, dreary month. One day, I got my guitar out and sat down and wrote an entire song. A song for Ned, for us, for what could have been. It was a simple song, with just a few basic cords, but it came off really well.

"Thank God for the rain
It's been a hot day
This Alabama soil needs the rain
As much as my lonesome heart needs you
Thank God for the rain
I forgot it was Sunday
Mama told me you'd stop by
She told me not to worry or to ask why
My little heart's lonesome
My deprivation is as dry
As the Earth on this hot southern day

But I shouldn't worry
You'll stop by soon
I know you will and I'll just sit and wait
And thank God for the rain
Thank God for the rain to
Wash away my pain
Thank God for the rain..."

I made a demo of the song, with me singing, and sent it to Jim. He said he was sure he could sell it, then congratulated me on writing it. I just said thanks and hung up the phone and wrote another song and then another. I was trying to purge all of my feeling onto the paper, to make myself whole again without Ned. It helped but it didn't take him away from me. The feelings were still there. I believed they would always be.

One night, I had gone to bed early, as I usually did those days, when I heard someone banging on the door. I didn't immediately think the obvious. For some reason, I thought it might be a burglar, though burglars rarely knock first.

Once I looked through the peephole, I saw it was Ned. He was standing there waiting for me to open the door.

"I know you're in there, Kori," he said. "Just open up. I want to talk to you."

I turned and felt a flush of feeling erupt through my body. But then it turned cold again. I opened the door and let him in without a word.

He came in, looked around, nodded and said, "You could have at least told me where you moved to."

"Why?" I mumbled.

"Because you ran out like a maniac and I was worried about you."

"How did you find me?"

"I called your ex-husband," he said. "He told me."

I nodded. "What do you want?"

"It's obvious, isn't it?"

"No, Ned, it's not obvious. Tell me what you want."

"You."

I shook my head and said, "You had me, now you don't. Isn't that why you want me? Because I don't want you?"

He stared at me, long and hard and said, "I don't know what kind of stupid game you're playing, but it's not working. I came here tonight because I want you to come home."

"I am home," I said.

"What do you want me to say?" he asked. "What do you want me to do? I'll do it. Just tell me."

I jerked my head at the door. "I want you to leave."

His face fell. He looked like he'd been hit in the stomach.

"I mean it, Ned," I said and went to the door. "I've done all I can do with what we had. I'm finally starting to get over you. Don't make this any harder than it already is."

"Kori," he said. "Why are you doing this? One day, you were fine and the next, you left."

"You know why."

"No, I don't!" he yelled, getting frustrated. "Tell me."

"Fine," I said. "I left because I realized you don't love me."

"Are you kidding me?" he snapped. "Are you kidding me with this?"

"No, I'm not."

"I don't love you?" he asked and shook his head like a madman. "What does it take for you?"

"It takes three words," I said. "That's what it takes."

He dropped his head again.

"But you can't say them," I said. "You can't do it. You can't feel it. Well, you know what? I loved you so much I gave up my life for you and to know that you couldn't be bothered to say it back, that hurt. It hurt a lot."

"But you know how I feel."

"No I don't! I don't know how you feel! I can't guess! I can't pretend!"

"Well, just so you'll know," he said and came over to me. "I do. I do love you, Kori. I always have."

"It's too late," I said.

"It's never too late," he told me and took my hand. "Let's give it another chance."

I shook my head and started to open the door. He stopped me and pushed it closed. I stepped back just as he held out his hand for me to take. I didn't take it. He dropped it.

"Why couldn't you say it before now?" I asked.

"Because," he said. "I thought if I said it, you wouldn't feel it anymore."

"What does that mean?"

"It means," he said and swallowed hard. "I thought if you knew how I felt, you would hurt me."

It made sense. If he gave me his heart, he'd lose something and that something would be control, control over our relationship and control over us. Over me.

This was so hard on him. He wasn't an overly emotional guy. What he gave, he gave between the sheets of our bed. That's how he communicated his love. He gave me his love; he didn't use words to convince me. He just gave it.

I stared at him, standing there, hurting over me. It made me hurt even more to have him look like that, with all this pain in his heart that showed in his eyes. I wanted to reach out to him so bad and take all that pain away. I wanted my pain to leave, too. But I'd given him so many chances to make things right with us. I couldn't do it anymore or I'd totally lose myself.

"I'm sorry, Ned," I said and opened the door. "But I can't do this anymore."

He didn't try to stop me. He didn't slam the door shut and he didn't cry out in pain. He, simply, nodded and walked through it and let me shut the door on us and our relationship and on everything we'd ever shared. And once I shut the door, I fell to the floor and began to sob. The sobs ripped out of my body and made me ache so bad I felt like I was being stabbed.

I looked around the apartment and realized I'd be here alone for a very long time. I realized I was lonely, even before I met Ned. I realized he'd made my life worth living. I realized he had given me his love. I just couldn't believe my luck at getting someone like him, someone who made the woman, the sexual being inside of me come out and roar. He meant so much to me and I was willing to throw all that away because of a grudge?

Oh, hell. Who was I fooling? I ran out after him. He was already in his truck, getting ready to pull out. As soon as he saw me, he began to smile. He knew he had me, that he had always had me. That was okay. I had him, too.

I stopped in front of his truck and he got out and came to me without a word. He bent down, brushed his lips against mine and I felt electric sparks fire up all inside me. I felt alive again. I felt freedom and joy and triumph. I felt love.

As the kiss deepened, I let everything go. All of the pain and the sadness and the confusion. I let everything go because my life was set straight again. And the reason it was set straight was because of him. He meant everything to me. I was never going to let him go again. At least not without a fight.

"I love you," I whispered in his ear. "I love you so much."

"I love you, too," he whispered back.

And I smiled because now, finally, I knew it was true. I would never doubt it again.

Lightning Source UK Ltd.
Milton Keynes UK
UKOW052150270612

195166UK00001B/72/P